Jinx

Cupid Cakes

'A deliciously enchanting
modern-day fairy tale'
Books Etc

'Witty and wicked, a brill read'
Mizz

'Devour the magic – hilarious
and a̶ ̶ ̶ ̶ ̶ ̶ ̶ ̶ ̶king'
Irish I̶ ̶ ̶

About the author

Fiona Dunbar began her career as an illustrator of children's books, as well as writing three picture books. But it was reading to her own children that inspired her to write her first novel, *The Truth Cookie*, closely followed by *Cupid Cakes* and *Chocolate Wishes* – which together make the hugely popular Lulu Baker trilogy (now filmed as Jinx for CBBC!). Since then Fiona has also written *Toonhead*, and the exciting Silk Sisters trilogy: *Pink Chameleon*, *Blue Gene Baby* and *Tiger-lily Gold.*

Fiona loves cooking almost as much as storytelling. With both, she tends to make things up as she goes along, and the result can sometimes be surprising! She lives in London with her husband and two children.

Jinx

Cupid Cakes

fiona dunbar

ORCHARD BOOKS

Thanks once again to all at Orchard, especially Ruth, my brilliant editor, as well as Ann-Janine, Goldy, and Mariesa and co. Thanks again to Hilary Delamere, and to Lee and Siobhan for all their support and brilliant insights. Thank you Aunty Cath, for being such a tireless fountain of knowledge. And thanks to all those kind, understanding people who forgive me for having my brain s   st of the time.

JF

ORCHARD BOOKS
338 Euston Road
London NW1 3BH
Orchard Books Australia
Hachette Children's Books Australia
Level 17/207 Kent Street, Sydney, NSW 2000

ISBN 978 1 40830 745 8

First published in Great Britain in 2005
This TV tie-in edition first published in 2009

A paperback original

Text © Fiona Dunbar 2005

The right of Fiona Dunbar to be identified as the author of
this work has been asserted by her in accordance with
the Copyright, Designs and Patents Act, 1988.
All rights reserved.

A CIP catalogue record for this book is available from the British Library.

1 3 5 7 9 10 8 6 4 2

Printed in Great Britain

Orchard Books is a division of Hachette Children's Books,
an Hachette UK company
www.hachette.co.uk

In loving memory of my Mum.
Also for Jane, who invented moonbathing,
and Karl, Holly and Ben.
F.D.

Contents

Cut an apple in half across its width. There, in each half, you will see a five-pointed star. Two stars: one represents Venus, the evening star, also known as Hesperus; the other is your star, the one which speaks to you, and only you, across time and space. Now imagine a magnificent garden surrounded by waters. It shares its name with Hesperus, which shines above it. In this garden are three nymphs, who guard a tree which bears golden apples. Very few people ever reach into that world and learn its secrets. You are one of them.

The first secret is this: anything and everything is possible.

The rest of the secrets that have been entrusted to me, I share with you in the following pages. Let your star guide you in using them.

From the introduction to *The Apple Star*,
by Ambrosia May

Magic Flower Juice

Cancer
June 22 – July 22

Hey, all you unadventurous crabs – this is no time to hide away in your shell! When the opportunity presents itself to help others, go for it – you know you *love* to be needed!!

Lulu Baker chucked the magazine down on the bed. Why do I read these things? she wondered. They were so annoying, and it was such a silly magazine...yet she never could quite resist. She lay back and gazed out of the skylight in her attic bedroom. What did she care for magazine horoscopes, anyway? She had her own personal star out there, and consulting it was her nightly habit now. The trouble was the growing sense of unease Lulu felt lately whenever she stared at it – this was what had made her consult her horoscope in the first place. Her star – the Truth Star, as she thought of it – still wasn't always easy to interpret; all she knew was that recently, gazing at it was giving her butterflies in her belly. Lulu picked up the little yellow bound book that lay beside her, and traced her finger over the gold star on its cover. Above it were the words:

The Apple Star
by
Ambrosia May

It was from this mysterious book that Lulu had learned all about her Truth Star, as well as many other fantastic secrets. It was, incredibly, a magic recipe book, and had fallen into her hands in mysterious circumstances on her thirteenth birthday. A message scrawled on the inside of the book's cover had seemed to suggest it was a gift from her mother...although Lulu could never be sure – her mother had died when Lulu was only five. But she still had her pictures of Mum, and now and then she found it reassuring to talk to them. She turned to her favourite picture now, the Mum-in-Muddy-Wellies one. But today, even this didn't seem to do the trick. Something was lurking around the corner, and neither Lulu's horoscope, nor the Truth Star, nor Mum-in-Muddy-Wellies could tell her what it was...

Lulu and her best friend, Frenchy, sat cross-legged on the dusty floor, their scripts in front of them, watching the two boys on stage. Mr Drinkmoore sat slumped like an oversized beanie toy on a chair nearby. Mr Drinkmoore had sad, red eyes that were too heavy for his face, so every now and then he had to squeeze his fingers under them to push them up. But they always slid back down again, even sadder and redder than before.

'Fetch me that flower,' one of the boys on stage enunciated breathlessly. 'The herb I showed thee once... The juice of it on sleeping eyelids...will make a man or woman madly dote...upon the next live creature that it sees.'

And the other boy piped up eagerly, 'I'll put a griddle around the Earth in forty minutes!'

'Aghh, William, William!' groaned Mr Drinkmoore, breaking off from a vigorous eye-squeezing. 'The word is *girdle*, not griddle! It's like a belt. You're a fairy; you're going to *fly around* the world in forty minutes, not *fry* it!'

'Blimey, sir. Not even a supersonic jet can do that!' quipped William.

This sent a ripple of giggles across the hall. 'Yes, yes, very...' *DINGALINGALING!* went the school bell. '...Amusing. Oh, go on, off you go.' There was a loud commotion as everyone began to gather up their things. Mr Drinkmoore stood up and bellowed over the din, 'And make sure you all practise your lines over the weekend!'

'This Shakespeare stuff's tricky, isn't it?' said Lulu, climbing to her feet. 'I'm glad I've only got a small part.' She and Frenchy had been cast as fairies.

'Me too,' said Frenchy, stretching out the long, thin, pale legs that her nickname, short for 'French Fry', described. She flicked back her equally long, thin, pale hair and stood up. 'Hey, and what about that love potion in the play! D'you think there really is such a flower?'

Lulu shot Frenchy a warning glance; she could tell where this conversation was leading. She marched purposefully towards the cloakroom.

Frenchy skipped to keep up with her. 'What's it called, "Love-in-Idleness"?' she went on. 'I've never heard of it, have you?'

Lulu stopped in her tracks and turned. 'Don't be ridiculous. It's just a story, Frenchy, you know that.' The moment she said it, though, doubt crept into her mind. If there was one thing she'd learned over the past eventful year, it was that every story had some truth in it!

But she knew where Frenchy was going with this; it

wasn't the first time she had dropped hints about *The Apple Star* and all its exciting possibilities, and Lulu didn't want to know. Lulu had used a recipe from *The Apple Star* just once, nearly a year ago, and ever since she had been, well, a little bit spooked by the whole business. She couldn't really explain why; after all, the one recipe she had used from it had been successful – far more so than she could ever have hoped. Dad had been about to marry Varaminta le Bone, a glamorous ex-model with a heart of steel. She and her spiteful son, Torquil, were making Lulu's life a misery at the time, but somehow they were always able to deceive Lulu's dad about what was really going on. When Lulu baked Ambrosia May's magical Truth Cookies, with their extraordinary ingredients, she had changed all that. Torquil ate them at the St Toast's school summer fair, and found himself strangely compelled to blurt out, very publicly, the truth about Varaminta's schemings against Lulu, how she was using Lulu's dad and how she had covered up Torquil's own nastiness. At last Lulu's dad had been able to see Varaminta for who she really was, and she and Torquil were out of their lives for ever. Even Aileen, their housekeeper and a close friend of Lulu's, was working for them again after she'd been sacked by Varaminta for no good reason. A nightmare had been brought to an end, and it was a recipe from

The Apple Star that had done it.

And yet, as special as *The Apple Star* was, Lulu felt uneasy: perhaps it was the new-found power that she found so unnerving. To think that all she had to do was use her secret recipes, and people would behave as she wished! It was all a bit too much to cope with.

'And I wish my mum would fall in love,' Frenchy went on, hinting for about the tenth time that week. 'She's been on her own too long; she even talks to herself. Remember in *The Apple Star*, how—'

'Shh!' hissed Lulu.

'Oops! Sorry, Lu.' Frenchy was quiet after that; she was the only friend Lulu had ever told about *The Apple Star*, and she knew perfectly well that it was top secret information. There had been a strict warning in the book about this, saying it was meant only for Lulu and no one else; that in the wrong hands, its recipes could be harmful. Lulu had bent the rules already, by telling Frenchy about it; no one else, not even Dad or Aileen, must know it existed. The fewer people who knew about it, however trustworthy they might be, the safer her little book and its powers would be.

So now the book spent most of the time languishing in its hiding place, unused since Lulu had made the Truth Cookies. Just occasionally, she would take it out and look at it, only to put it away again swiftly. There was a whole recipe section, she remembered, entitled 'Matters of the Heart'; something that clearly had a hold on Frenchy's imagination right now. Helped along, no doubt, by the school production of *A Midsummer Night's Dream*.

'Look, French,' said Lulu, as soon as they were alone. 'You're out of your mind if you think I'm going to start mucking about, making people fall in love with each other. No way, n'uh-uh, way too risky, the book says as much. It's serious stuff! So don't even think about it, OK?'

Frenchy sighed. 'You're right. Oh well. I've no idea who we'd pair my mum off with anyway.'

But even though Lulu was convinced she was right, the words from her horoscope, 'unadventurous crabs', kept going around in her head on the way home. Must stop reading those stupid things, she told herself.

Concrete Quiche

On the top deck of the bus to Camden Town, Frenchy and Lulu plopped themselves into seats close to the front. It was a brilliant Sunday afternoon in May, and they were on their way to the zoo with Frenchy's mum, Jill. Lulu was busy searching her pocket for bubblegum, when Frenchy suddenly grabbed her shoulder.

'It's her!' Frenchy said in a loud whisper, nodding at the woman in front of them.

Bewildered, Lulu studied the back of the woman's head, trying to work out if she recognised her. Then Frenchy nudged and pointed, and Lulu realised that it was not the woman herself Frenchy was talking about, but her magazine. It was obviously a gossip magazine, full of glossy pictures of glossy people. Lulu shifted closer to get a good look. Then she felt a hot little explosion in her belly. There, grinning from a page in the magazine, with her shimmery hair, silvery jewels, silky dress and silly dog, was Lulu's evil almost-stepmother: Varaminta le Bone.

In a second she was gone as the page flipped over. The two girls sighed loudly with frustration.

Throughout the journey, Lulu craned her neck forward in the hope that the woman would return to the article about Varaminta. But she didn't. Then, just as they were approaching their stop, the woman's head lolled forward and she nodded off. The magazine slid onto the seat next to her. Brilliant! thought Lulu and, seizing her chance, she snatched the magazine up just as Jill was saying, 'OK, come on, girls!'

Jill was an interesting person to go to the zoo with, probably because she was a teacher. She always had something different to say about the animals, like, 'Did you know it's the *male* seahorse that carries the babies,' or, 'The sloth is so hard of hearing, you could fire a gun by his ear and all he'd do is turn and blink!' Lulu often thought how nice it would be to have Jill as her teacher, rather than the weary Mr Drinkmoore, or boring Miss Broccoli. But much as she liked Jill, Lulu was desperate to get away from her for once, so she could sneak a look at the magazine which she had slipped discreetly into her backpack. She hoped to get an opportunity at lunchtime.

'Quiche?' offered Jill, as they settled themselves at a picnic bench.

Lulu watched as Jill cut off an enormous wedge,

which landed on its paper plate with a thud. The 'quiche' had a great fat concrete crust, and jellyish green bits inside.

'Er...no, thanks,' said Lulu. 'Got my sandwich!' She was relieved that, for once, she didn't have to consume one of Jill's creations. Whenever she had supper at Frenchy's house it was always slithery aubergines or rubbery tofu, accompanied by some gritty, stringy greens from Jill's allotment that she apparently never quite managed to wash properly.

'Is that Jill?' said a man's voice.

They all looked up. The man who had spoken was a very pale person, made to look even paler by his very black clothes. His polo-neck sweater and leather jacket were black, and he had a big, battered, white book squished into his pocket. He wore narrow, rectangular black-framed glasses, a miniature grey ponytail and a tiny triangle of beard. He looked as if he'd stepped out of a black-and-white movie.

'Oh, *hi*!' said Jill who, by contrast, was very much in colour, her bright red face clashing with her green jumper. 'Gosh, *hi*! How *are* you? It's been a long time...'

The man nodded and said something that sounded like, 'Yaahs'.

'Gosh,' said Jill again. 'Well, we were just having some lunch...I mean, *obviously*! Are you...have you...?'

'Eaten? No!' said the man.

'Would you...?' said Jill.

'Love to!' said the man, at exactly the same time. The two of them laughed nervously. Lulu and Frenchy looked at each other, and rolled their eyes heavenward.

Jill introduced Frenchy, by her real name – Amanda. Then she introduced Lulu.

'Basil Larsenbarsen,' said the man, holding out a hand. 'Pleased to meet you.' He pronounced 'Basil' to rhyme with 'nasal'. Which was exactly how his voice sounded.

'We used to teach at the same school,' added Jill. 'Are you still...?'

'Oh, NEAUOO!' said Basil Larsenbarsen, seating himself next to her. 'Oi am, Oi can rapturously report, now working on moy *magnum opus*.'

Lulu, finishing her sandwich, heard only the word 'magnum'. 'Ooh, yum, I wouldn't mind one of those!' she said.

Frenchy nudged her. 'It's not an ice cream, silly!'

Jill chuckled. 'It's Latin,' she explained. 'It means "great work". Quiche?' She turned to Basil with the plate.

'What sort of great work?' asked Frenchy.

Basil Larsenbarsen couldn't answer for a moment, as his teeth were cemented together by Jill's wholemeal pastry. 'Mmm...hnn. Oi'm...unn...wroiting a novel. That's woy Oi'm here...research.'

Frenchy wiped her mouth with her napkin. 'Well, it's nice to meet you,' she said. 'We're going to have a wander...see you in a bit, Mum?'

Lulu jumped up eagerly.

'OK,' said Jill. 'I'll join you in a few minutes, all right, love?'

The girls sped off. The moment they rounded the corner beside the gorilla enclosure, Lulu pulled out the magazine. Only now did she see its cover.

'Oh, it's *Chow!* magazine!' she said. 'Of course! Remember, she was planning this when she was with my dad?'

'Oh, I remember all right,' said Frenchy. 'She couldn't wait to show off the engagement ring, the house and everything...except you.'

They found the page with Varaminta's interview. Lulu couldn't suppress a malicious chuckle. 'Only one page! Remember when it was going to be seven?'

'Serves her right!' remarked Frenchy.

The picture showed Varaminta lounging with Poochie, her deranged doglet, on a couch in front of a gigantic flower arrangement. The girls fell silent as they read the interview together. Most of it was extremely boring. Then they came to the interesting part. Lulu felt a little thrill at the mention of her father's name.

Chow: You recently separated from your fiancé [advertising executive Michael Baker]. How are you adjusting?

Varaminta le Bone: I am rebuilding my life as best I can. I have the loving support of my darling son, Torquil, and close friends. I can't say too much about this...but in time the truth will be known about what happened. All I can say now is that *someone* deliberately set out to destroy our relationship.

Chow: Another woman?

Varaminta le Bone: In a manner of speaking, yes – a very...*young* woman. I have *evidence* of foul play, and let me tell you, I don't take these things lying down.

Chow: You mean you intend to have your revenge?

Varaminta le Bone: Oh, yes. She's going to pay for this. And love will reign supreme once again. But I don't really want to talk about that. My book, *How To Be As Thin As Me* is, after some delay, out now in paperback...

The rest of the piece was about Varaminta's book. Lulu, wide-eyed, gaped at Frenchy.

Frenchy stared gravely back. 'A very young woman? Lu, she means you.'

All the commotion of the zoo – the screaming toddlers, the giggling teenagers, the whoops and cries of the animals – seemed to fade away for a moment as the horror and pain of her time with the le Bones came flooding back to Lulu. Varaminta's eyes glinted at her from the magazine page with their familiar malice. Even that sickening perfume of Varaminta's seemed to drift up from her picture and squeeze at Lulu's throat. Lulu coughed, and tears pricked at her eyes. Mingled with animal-pong, the smell began to make her feel nauseous. She moved away from the gorillas, almost colliding with a zoo keeper coming the other way with a cart of cleaning things, and dropping the magazine at the same time.

'Watch it, love,' warned the zoo keeper.

'Sorry,' muttered Lulu as she headed for a nearby bench.

Frenchy rushed after her. 'Hey, are you all right, Lu?'

Lulu took a deep breath. 'Yeah, I think so. Just felt a bit sick...think I'll rest here for a bit.' This is it, she thought; this was why she'd had such a heavy sense of foreboding every time she'd looked at the Truth Star recently – it had to be some kind of warning.

They sat quietly for a moment. Suddenly, Frenchy smiled and said, 'Well, if it's any consolation, I think your friend Varaminta's getting ripped to shreds. Take a look over there.'

Lulu looked up. The magazine, which must have found its way into the enclosure via the zoo keeper's cart, was being torn and tossed about by a young gorilla. Lulu, feeling slightly better, managed a little chuckle. Then the gorilla picked up a scrap of the shredded magazine, sniffed it, bared its teeth in a look of sheer disgust, and threw it out of the enclosure. The scrap landed by Lulu's feet; she picked it up. It was a tiny bottle of perfume, a free sample stuck to an advertisement. Lulu realised it must have been this perfume that she'd smelled coming from the magazine pages. A shred of paper was still stuck to the back of the bottle, and on it was Varaminta's face.

'Uh-oh, "Je Reviens",' said Frenchy.

'What?' said Lulu.

'It's the name of that perfume. "Je Reviens"; it's French. It means, "I shall return".'

Apple Characters

'How was the zoo?' asked Dad.

Lulu trailed behind him into the kitchen. 'Oh, fine,' she replied, half-heartedly. She suddenly felt very tired but resisted the urge to go and turn on the TV. She knew Dad had been working alone at home all day, even though it was the weekend, and wanted to chat.

'Supper's almost ready,' said Dad, turning on the burner under the wok. 'Take a look at those ideas of mine, I want your opinion,' he added, jerking his head in the direction of some rough drawings he had left on the kitchen table.

Lulu slumped into a kitchen chair and stared blankly at the drawings.

'They're for this new client of ours, the English Apple Marketing Board,' Dad went on.

Lulu sifted vaguely through the drawings, trying to take an interest. 'Why'd you need to advertise apples?'

'*English* apples,' Dad corrected. 'Because a lot of

them are in danger of extinction while we have other, less interesting ones flown in from the other side of the planet.'

'I never thought apples could become extinct.'

'Well, it's true,' said Dad, throwing some colourful vegetables into the wok. 'There are all these varieties I'd never heard of! Only, they have an image problem. Would you eat a William Crump, for instance?'

Lulu wrinkled her nose.

'So anyway,' he went on, 'those are some apple characters I've been inventing. How do you like Pixie; isn't she cute? And D'Arcy Spice just *had* to be a dashing nineteenth century gent...'

But Lulu's mind was elsewhere. She couldn't stop thinking about Varaminta, and she wondered whether or not to tell Dad about the *Chow!* magazine article. It was unlikely he had seen it already, and right now she felt as if she might need his protection. 'Dad...' she ventured.

Dad squirted some sauce at the wok, which hissed and steamed angrily. He rocked it this way and that as he energetically stir-fried its contents. 'Yup?' he shouted above the din.

On the other hand, thought Lulu, what on earth would Dad make of Varaminta's remarks about the '*evidence* of foul play'? Lulu didn't know exactly what it meant herself, but drawing attention to it would only raise all sorts of questions in Dad's mind, and the last thing she wanted was for him to find out about the Truth Cookies or *The Apple Star*. No, best not to mention it. 'Oh...never mind,' she said at last.

Dad slooshed the steaming mixture into two bowls, and carried them to the table. 'Grub's up!'

Lulu shifted the drawings aside to make room for her bowl. 'Dad,' she said eventually, deciding to tackle the other thing that was worrying her.

'Mmm?' said Dad, slurping his noodles.

'You'd never...' She trailed off, losing her nerve. 'By the way,' she said, changing the subject. 'Frenchy's mum told me to tell you there's a party a week on Tuesday. It's at an art gallery – you know Frenchy's dad's an artist? Well, it's his first one-man show...I'm invited, and she wondered if you might like to go as well?' Lulu found her voice growing a little too loud, a little too bright, as she endeavoured to cover up what she was really thinking.

Dad gave Lulu a sideways look. 'I'll...check my diary.' He moved closer and stared her straight in the eye. 'Now will you tell me what's on your mind. Come on, out with it! I'd never...what?'

Lulu shifted her gaze to her bowl as she said in a small voice, 'You'd never get back together with Varaminta, would you?'

Dad half choked on his mouthful, and took a swig of beer. 'No foul language at the dinner table, please! Of course not. Ugh! Whatever made you think of such a thing? You'll put me right off my food.'

Lulu laughed. 'Sorry, Dad.' Then she couldn't help adding, 'If I...that is, if someone... Say if there was this person, right? And this person wanted to...get me.'

'Get you?' Dad looked worried. 'Are you being bullied?'

'No! That is...'

'Who's this "person", then?'

'Oh, no one in particular.'

'Ah, I get it,' said Dad. 'You've seen her, haven't you!'

'Seen her?'

'I saw her too.'

Lulu's noodles slithered off her fork. 'You did?' Oh boy, she thought; what if he'd read the article? Could he have made a connection between Varaminta's comments and Lulu herself?

'Yes,' Dad continued. 'In the bookshop. I walked past it the other day; her book was in the window. Ha! I wondered when it would come out. I heard it had been delayed because the hardback sold so poorly...'

'Oh, yes!' Lulu heaved a sigh of relief. 'That's it. I saw the book.'

Dad leaned over and put his arm around her shoulder. 'Noodle, you have nothing to fear from that woman. Or her poisonous son. Nobody's going to "get" you, understand? Whatever's made you think that? Now eat up, and tell me about the zoo.'

*

Lulu went to bed elated that night. I'm so silly, she thought. Fancy thinking Dad could be taken in by Varaminta all over again, after all that had happened! Now she knew for certain that no matter how convinced Varaminta was that she could win him back (which certainly seemed to be what she was hinting at in the interview, with all that 'love will reign supreme once again' nonsense), Dad would not be playing ball. And if Varaminta were to try anything on Lulu, Dad would protect her.

Lulu peered out of her bedroom skylight in search of her Truth Star. She half expected that the uneasy feeling would be gone now when she saw it. Perhaps the worst was over, she told herself; that nasty reminder of Varaminta had been all it was about, and her empty threats would amount to nothing anyway. But the sky was filled with cloud; she would be unable to consult her star tonight. Lulu found herself turning to her Wodge of Stuff instead. The Wodge was her personal store of mementoes of Mum, wrapped in an elastic band and stored in an old cake tin. Mum-in-Muddy-Wellies used to be in there too, before taking pride of place on Lulu's bedside table. Lulu picked out another picture of Mum, in a meadow of wild flowers. How very different from the artifice of Varaminta's picture in *Chow!* magazine, posed before that artful flower arrangement. Lulu gazed at the Mum-in-a-Meadow picture and thought about Varaminta's interview, and what else it might mean. What on earth was this 'evidence' Varaminta claimed to have? Lulu couldn't imagine what it might be, but the longer she stared at her mum's picture, the more unsettled she became. No matter how hard she tried to stop them, the words kept going round and round in her head; Varaminta knows something.

Lulu shivered.

Basil and Broccoli

A boy and a girl stood on the stage. 'Tempt not too much the hatred of my spirit,' said the boy, pushing the girl aside. '...For I am *sick* when I do look on thee!'

'And I am sick when I look *not* on you,' whimpered the girl.

'Oh boy!' sighed Lulu, stretching wearily. 'This is taking *ages*!'

'Yeah, but stay awake, Lu,' said Frenchy, propping her up. 'Our scene's next.'

Lulu groaned. 'I hardly slept all night. How much does Varaminta know, French?'

'I've been wondering about that too,' whispered Frenchy. 'If she knows it was you who made Torquil spill the beans about her nasty schemes, then does she know about the Truth Cookies? And if she knows about the cookies, does that mean she knows about *The Apple Star*?'

'Will you be quiet back there!' barked Mr Drinkmoore.

After what felt like an age, the rehearsal came to an end, and it was time to go home. 'Hiya, kid, how you doing!' said Aileen, chucking Lulu affectionately under the chin as she met the girls at the school gates. 'Hey, French. I got a call from your mum; you're coming back with us for a while, OK? She's meeting a friend after school. A last minute arrangement or something.'

Frenchy stood still and put her hands on her hips. 'Male or female?'

'Ooh, get you!' said Aileen, slapping her gently on the arm. 'She didn't say. Someone she used to teach with or something. Bumped into them at the zoo?'

Lulu and Frenchy stared at each other, wide-eyed. 'Oh, good grief!' cried Frenchy. 'Not that *Bay*-zil creep! He's *awful*!'

Lulu chuckled. 'What was that name? Bayzil Larsen-Farsen-Arsen-Barsen?'

'Steady on!' interrupted Aileen. 'Poor guy can't help having a funny name, y'know!'

'You haven't met him!' Frenchy almost shrieked. 'He talks like he's got a clothes peg on his nose and he's just eaten something revolting: "Oi'm wroiting moy magnum opus."'

'Come on, French, she does have a point,' said Lulu. 'You were just saying how lonely your mum is. Then as soon as she goes on a date, you don't like it! He might be all right, you hardly know him. He was gone by the time we joined your mum again; we only met him for a minute.'

'Lulu's right, French,' added Aileen. But one corner of her mouth curled up. 'Though I must admit he does sound like a bit of a prat!'

'See!' retorted Frenchy, shoving Lulu.

*

In a vast hall hung with masterpieces from floor to ceiling, Miss Broccoli stood beside a portrait of an elegant Spanish lady and waited for the group to settle. Lulu usually enjoyed school outings, and had been looking forward to this one. But as Miss Broccoli began to talk about the painting, her attention soon gave way to the anxious thoughts that had been plaguing her since she'd seen the *Chow!* article. All she could think of was those threatening words of Varaminta's; what if she really did know about *The Apple Star*, and had resolved to steal it? Lulu had a new hiding place for it, under a loose floorboard. A good spot, if all she was counting on was Dad and Aileen not seeing it. But now her imagination was running wild and she pictured Torquil skiving off school to break into the house. He'd surely find it, and who knew what evil doings the two le Bones would be capable of, with those recipes in their hands? Lulu made a mental note to hide the book somewhere less predictable. At that moment, her eye was caught by a figure who had just entered the room. A chill ran through her as she realised that the funny-looking, bearded man with tinted glasses had followed their group to every room so far. Was he spying on her? He turned to look at her, and she quickly looked away, her heart thumping. She could have sworn she'd seen him somewhere before, too. Well, if Varaminta wanted to wreak revenge, or get to *The Apple Star,* then having Lulu followed would be a logical place to start, wouldn't it? Maybe he'd even been hired by Varaminta to *kidnap* her?! Or was she just being paranoid?

Lulu stared intently at the portrait Miss Broccoli was lecturing them about. '...and the *Lady with a Fan* is a good example of this. Watch as you walk past,' she said, 'and you will notice how the eyes follow you around the room.'

Eyes, eyes...staring from holes in portraits, peering through keyholes, following her around the room, following her down the road...oh, help! It was all too much. It was a situation which called for chocolate but, as usual, Lulu didn't have the £1.25 for the brick of Belgian stuff they always seemed to have in museum shops. She settled instead for a postcard of the Spanish lady portrait.

Frenchy joined her at the queue for the till. 'There you are! Listen, let's make sure we sit together on the coach going back, OK? We need to talk. Old Windbag hasn't let up for a nanosecond, has she?'

'Yeah, sorry about this morning,' said Lulu glumly. 'I was late; only just caught the coach so I had to sit up front near Broccoli, it was so boring.'

'Well, make sure you find me on the way back,' said Frenchy urgently.

*

Lulu and Frenchy steered past the gaggle of girls they would usually have joined on the coach. They also took care to give bully Zena Lemon and her gang a wide berth – they were to be avoided at all times. 'Over here,' said Frenchy at last, finding a seat close to the boys that she knew would allow them some privacy, engrossed as they were in their card games.

'Listen, Lu. Mum's got another date with that creep,' whispered Frenchy, as they settled into their seats. 'This Saturday night!'

'What, Bay-zil Larsen-Farsen-Arsen-Barsen?' said Lulu. But Frenchy didn't laugh, and Lulu felt irritation once again as she saw where this was leading. 'Look, French, I really don't think I can help. And anyway, it's not right to go meddling in other people's business for no good reason.'

'I can think of a very good reason!' said Frenchy, chewing her gum furiously.

Lulu put her hands on her hips. 'Uh, hello? Who's got the *real* problems around here? *I'm* terrified Varaminta's on my tail and my...book's going to get stolen, or she'll have me kidnapped, or something!' The boys across the aisle looked up from their Top Trumps game. 'And you—'

'Sshh!' hissed Frenchy. 'Look, I was coming to that...' She glanced at the boys and waited.

Lulu stared crossly out of the window at the rain-sodden traffic. When the boys resumed their game, Frenchy tugged Lulu's sleeve. 'Lu, what I was going to say was, I've thought of a way I can help you – at least a bit – as well as you helping me.'

Lulu still stared out of the window, but felt her ears prick up. 'How's that, then?' she said at last.

'Lu, have you ever thought about your dad and my mum?'

Lulu turned to face her. 'What do you mean?'

'I mean...' Frenchy drew closer and whispered. 'Like you once said, wouldn't it be great if we were sisters. *Your dad and my mum!*'

Lulu gasped. A whole shop window of possibilities suddenly opened up in front of her. Sharing a room with

Frenchy, talking until the moon was high. Dad and Jill, holding hands and gazing adoringly at each other. A Sunday stroll in the park, the four of them laughing together. She remembered her horoscope, with its words about an opportunity to help someone. This was it! The whole idea was so ludicrously perfect, like a picture postcard. It was outrageous and simple and lovely. She could think of nothing bad about it at all, from anyone's point of view. Well, maybe one thing.

'Oh, French, I'd have to eat your mum's food!'

'Hey! You should try being a vegetarian,' said Frenchy, indignantly. 'Everything we grow in the allotment is organic, and—'

'OK, I know,' chuckled Lulu, waving this aside. 'All right, now I get it. And apart from making your mum and my dad happy, it might help keep Varaminta's scheming nose out of things. It's bound to make it harder for her to try to win Dad back or have her revenge on me, isn't it?'

'Exactly,' said Frenchy. 'And if Mum and I are around at your place a lot, that's added protection for you and the book as well.'

'But hang on, we have to think this through carefully,' said Lulu. 'This is a big thing. A huge thing!'

Frenchy grabbed her hand. 'I know, but it's brilliant, isn't it?'

Recipe for Disaster

Your dad and my mum...Lulu was still thinking about it when she got home. Perhaps it *was* a brilliant idea, she thought as she headed upstairs. Mums and dads seemed all too capable of making disastrous choices when it came to partners: look at who Dad chose last time. How could she be sure the next one wouldn't be just as awful? At least if she could get him to fall for Jill, she would know what she was getting. 'Better the devil you know, than the devil you don't', as Dad would say. Lulu always used to think that was a daft thing to say, like, 'Better to eat something you know is poison, than something that might not be'. But now she understood that it was all about how much easier it was to deal with the imperfections in people that you were used to, than those you weren't. Which was exactly why fixing her dad up with Jill made so much sense; as far as Lulu could see, her only imperfection was her cooking. Who knew? Maybe she could even come to like that, too. She would never replace Mum, of course – nobody could – but Lulu really did like her.

Lulu mused on all of this as she took the postcard of the Spanish lady portrait out of her bag. Her eyes fixed for a moment on the stare of the woman in the picture. But as she pinned the postcard to her noticeboard, she realised that she hadn't had to move the pile of books usually in front of the board to do so. Strange; had Aileen snuck in and tidied up while she was out? No; there was just as much clutter on her desk as usual, but everything seemed to have been shoved into the middle. Lulu felt the blood drain from her face as she was seized with a horrible certainty; someone had been in her room...and they had been looking for something...

The Apple Star! She dashed across the room, to the place where the carpet pulled up easily, and lifted the loose floorboard: it was still there. She picked it up and hugged it, letting out a gasp of relief. 'Thank goodness!'

She was sure she'd been lucky this time; the intruder had probably left in a hurry. It was the only possible explanation as to why they hadn't found her stupid, obvious hiding place. Everyone in stories, who ever had something special to hide, *always* stuck it under a loose floorboard! He or she must have got as far as the desk, then probably been interrupted. They hadn't even had time to put things back as they were. Lulu checked – the

Wodge of Stuff was all present and correct inside its tin, thankfully. Well, of course, it wouldn't have made any sense to interfere with that; there was just one thing the intruder was interested in. Now her thoughts were running around in her head and bumping into each other. 'Does she know about the Truth Cookies?' went Frenchy's voice. '...And if she knows about the cookies, does that mean she knows about *The Apple Star*?' Well, clearly she did. It had to be Varaminta – or someone acting on her behalf. But how? What on earth had made Varaminta connect the change in Torquil's behaviour, when he'd come out with all those truths about himself and his mother, to the cookies he'd eaten and a magical recipe book? Lulu gazed out of the skylight and wished it was night and the Truth Star was there to help her right now. Somewhere in the recesses of her mind, Lulu had an ominous sense that there was something that could have helped Varaminta to make this connection...or was it some*one*? Then it hit her: Grodmila.

It was Grodmila, Varaminta's mean-spirited and cabbage-obsessed replacement for Aileen, who had seen Lulu making the cookies without knowing what they really were; she had even put *The Apple Star* away, after Lulu had left the book in the kitchen by mistake. She had actually touched it! Lulu hadn't worried about it too much at the time as Grodmila, recently arrived from

Grizlonia, could barely understand a word of English. She couldn't have read the recipes even if she'd wanted to. But now...what if Grodmila was still working for Varaminta? Nearly a year had passed; her English was bound to have improved. An image presented itself in Lulu's mind, of Varaminta sitting behind a large desk, like in an old spy film; Torquil standing to attention at her side. 'Tell me everything you know about what happened that day!' she would demand. And Secret Agent Grodmila would smirk triumphantly: 'I hev some information I think you vill find very eenteresting...'

This was the missing ingredient that Lulu had been searching for; the 'evidence' Varaminta claimed to have. Lulu wasn't being paranoid at all – Varaminta and Torquil knew about *The Apple Star* and were out to get it!

'Lulu!' called Aileen from downstairs. 'Supper's ready!'

Lulu put her precious book back under the floorboard; she'd have to think of somewhere new for it later. Grimly, she headed downstairs.

As Lulu passed the open door to the living room, she noticed the chandelier was missing. She went into the room, and saw that the big, heavy swags of curtain that had shrouded the windows only that morning were gone as well. The room looked naked, the way it always did after the Christmas decorations first came down.

Aileen appeared in the doorway. 'How about that, eh?

Back to normal at last!'

Lulu stared at the bare windows, perplexed.

'The movers came today, remember?' said Aileen. 'Took the last of you-know-who's stuff.'

'Oh, good grief.'

'I thought I told you...what's up, kiddo?'

'Oh, it's nothing, I...I'd forgotten.'

'Yeah, remember your dad agreed to hang on to a few things till Varaminta got her own place sorted. Well, she has at last. I guess it has been a few months.'

'Hey, don't tell me you liked all that stuff?' said Aileen. 'No way!'

'And don't you remember there was that big stack of pictures in the corner, Varaminta's fashion shots...'

'Oh, of course,' said Lulu, noticing the empty space. 'But...you were here, right? Er, did the movers go into my room at all?'

'I wouldn't have thought so. There wasn't any of her stuff in there, surely?'

Lulu paused; no point in harping on about it. Suppose Varaminta had tried to get the movers to steal the book: they hadn't succeeded. Besides, what could she say? 'No, of course not,' she said eventually. 'So that's it then, is it? They don't need to come back for anything else?'

'No, that's the lot. Come on, let's eat.'

Giant Gobstoppers

'You never know though, they might have stolen a spare key,' said Frenchy. 'They still might come back. Or they might break in.'

Lulu stared into space, as once again she contemplated the possibility of *The Apple Star* being stolen.

'You walking towards the bus stop?' asked Frenchy.

'Oh, yeah,' said Lulu vaguely. 'Got piano,' she added, waving her music bag. Lulu's new piano teacher lived near to the school, so every Wednesday she walked round for her lesson. They set off together.

Frenchy peered at Lulu. 'Sorry, Lu, didn't mean to freak you out.'

'I know. You're right, though,' said Lulu. 'I need to get back in touch with Cassandra.' It was Cassandra – big, fabulous, exotic Cassandra – who had supplied Lulu with all the very unusual ingredients for the Truth Cookies from the depths of her spice-scented treasure-trove, and who had been brimming over with valuable information and advice on *The Apple Star* and its magic. 'You know, I was thinking about something she once said. I'd asked her to make the Truth Cookies *for* me, but she said no, it wouldn't work; they had to be made *by* me. So surely that means the recipes wouldn't work for Varaminta, either?'

'Hmmm,' said Frenchy, chewing vigorously on her piece of gum. 'But, Lu, what about the warning in the book? About the recipes being harmful in the wrong hands?'

'We-ell, that's true, but...how come Cassandra said that, then?'

Frenchy popped a bubble. 'I dunno, perhaps she just meant it wouldn't work in the same *way*.'

Lulu groaned. 'Oh, you're probably right. Now I think of it, Cassandra did say something about it "backfiring" if it wasn't me who made the cookies. That could be even worse.'

'"The cook's the most important ingredient," as my mum would say,' added Frenchy. 'But anyway, I wouldn't worry too much about Varaminta getting hold of the book; even if she had a key, she'd still have to be dead careful about being caught by Aileen or someone.'

'Hey, you two!' said a voice. It was Galinda

Gudvitsa, or Glynnie for short. Glynnie was a classic Indian beauty, all glossy hair, big expressive eyes and brilliant teeth. Talented and brainy, too; a goddess, in short. Lulu had always admired her, yet been too shy to befriend her until she'd noticed Glynnie's tendency towards clumsiness. This had brought her down to a mortal level in Lulu's eyes, and when she'd got to know Glynnie, she'd found that she was funny, warm and not in the least bit proud. Lulu often thought of people in terms of what they might be like if they were some kind of sweet. She had eventually decided that Glynnie was like that sophisticated, adult, after-dinner chocolate that seemed to pronounce itself as too special for her, until she ate it and found she actually liked it.

'Hey, Glyn, learned all your lines yet?' said Frenchy, hastily changing the subject as Glynnie approached them. Glynnie, unsurprisingly, had landed the part of Titania, queen of the fairies, in the play.

'No way!' said Glynnie, adding in a whisper, 'and – oops, sorry!' she said, as she tripped over Lulu's shoe '– I'm thinking of divorcing my husband!' Frenchy giggled; everyone knew that the boy playing Oberon the fairy king had only got the part because of his pushy mother, and couldn't act to save his life.

'Ooh, look, little Miss Good-Witch has got a secret!'

sneered Zena Lemon, who had come up alongside them. Zena and her sidekick Chantrelle Portobello cast a heavy shadow before them. Their sweaters stretched strenuously around their lumpen middles, while their tiny skirts shrivelled away from their massive thighs like burst sausage skins. They were both as tall as they were broad, with shoulders slunk into a permanent, disdainful stoop. Despite this, they clearly enjoyed towering over everyone, their height enhanced by platform shoes roughly the size and shape of breeze blocks. These were the 'Zena's Gang' hallmarks, together with rings like knuckle-dusters, huge hooped earrings and a helmet of heavily-gelled hair. These girls were big. They were heavy. They were *hard*! Only one sweet could begin to describe them: gobstoppers.

'Ooh, what's your secret, oh pleeeze tell!' Zena went on. 'Is it – ah, I know, "I'm going to stay up extwa late learning my lines, 'cos I weally want to make Mr Dwinkmaw happy".' Zena fluttered her eyelashes sarcastically.

Glynnie stared at the pavement and picked up the pace. Frenchy and Lulu walked close to her on either side, forming a protective barrier. Zena and her gang could get really nasty, and things had got worse for Glynnie since she had landed the most coveted role in the play.

'"…'Cos I just *love* Mr Dwinkmaw",' Zena went on, '"and—"'

'Gosh, how did you guess!' Frenchy interrupted suddenly. 'We're going to do the same, too!'

'Actually, I'm not even going to bed tonight,' said Lulu, deciding to join in. 'I love Shakespeare sooo much, I'm going to stay up and learn everyone else's part as well as my own!'

All Zena could manage in return was a hostile squint that made her mascara'd eyes look like two scrunched-up spiders. 'Hur-hur.'

Then Chantrelle Portobello pitched in. 'Don't she talk for herself, eh? Got to have her mates do all the talking for her, innit!'

Zena raised a heavily-plucked eyebrow in recognition of Chantrelle's clever tactical shift. 'Ye-eah, wot about it, Good Witch? Got anyfink to say for yourself? Or are ya too busy spouting Shakespeare to fink of any words of your own?'

Glynnie stopped in her tracks and turned. 'Yes, you're absolutely right. So how about this: methinks you stinks, thou gleeking cankerblossom!'

This brought loud whoops and yelps of enjoyment from onlookers, which made Zena turn purple with rage. She raised her arm to give Glynnie a good clout, but her hand was stayed by Jake Hershey, the heartthrob of 8B, who had just caught up with them.

'Now now, girls,' said Jake, cool as cream.

Zena melted visibly at the sight of him, and particularly at the touch of his hand on hers. She gazed swooningly into his eyes as she lowered her arm. 'I wa'n't gonna hit her or nuffink,' she said. 'We was just 'aving a laugh.'

'Right,' said Jake, narrowing his eyes at her as he extracted his hand from her vice-like grip. He snuck a sideways, admiring peek at Glynnie.

Zena waited until he had moved on, then hissed at Glynnie, 'I'm gonna get you.' Chantrelle Portobello threw in a snarl, for good measure, and the two flounced off ahead.

By now they had reached the bus stop. 'OK, guys, see you tomorrow,' said Lulu. She exchanged glances with Glynnie and rolled her eyes. Glynnie smiled back, as if to say, 'I can handle it.'

''Bye,' said Frenchy. 'Hope you sort out...that thing.'

'Thanks,' said Lulu, and turned off the main street into the cul-de-sac where her piano teacher lived. Away from the traffic, the street's calm hush was interrupted only by the clatterings of a solitary boy, as he practised flips on his skateboard. Lulu realised she and Frenchy hadn't even had a chance to discuss the

Dad and Jill plan, with all that had been going on. She would need to consult *The Apple Star* for recipes too. Well, with half-term coming up next week, there would be plenty of time for that.

Lulu wandered towards the piano teacher's house lost in thought, then the sound of fast approaching wheels made her look up and she saw that the boy on the skateboard was racing straight towards her. Lulu backed up against the wall as, with a flourish, the boy came to a halt right in front of her. 'Well well, fancy meeting you here!' he said.

'Torquil!' gasped Lulu. 'What are you doing here?'

'What's the matter, aren't you pleased to see me?' said Torquil, with that familiar smirk of his. His face was longer and leaner than it had been a year ago, but the gleam in his eye from beneath the floppy fringe was just as malevolent.

Lulu's hands felt clammy. 'No!' she snapped, with all the confidence she could muster. 'And I'm going to be late for my piano lesson, so if you'll excuse me...' She tried to walk around him.

Torquil jumped in her path. 'Uh-uh! His other pupil hasn't even come out yet. And you and I have important business to discuss. About the recipe book.'

Lulu hoped she looked perplexed. 'What recipe book?'

'Ha ha, very good!' Torquil clapped his hands slowly. 'Think you might change your tune, though, when you hear what I've got to say.'

'I'm not changing any tune, now get out of my way!' Lulu tried to push past him.

Torquil grabbed her arm. 'You could do very well out of that, you know. You could make millions!'

Oh, here we go, thought Lulu. She hadn't even considered Torquil's angle on all this; it figured that something as special as *The Apple Star* would make his eyes light up with greed. That was Torquil all over.

Lulu struggled, and Torquil tightened his grip. 'You help me get to it, and I could help you,' he went on. 'On the other hand, we could just take the book anyway. But if that happens, I'm afraid you won't get a cut in the deal. Your loss.'

'I don't know what you're talking about!' Lulu insisted. She yanked her arm free and ran on.

Torquil jumped back on the skateboard and caught up with her. He circled her as he went on. '...We *will* get it, you know. It'd be easier if you helped – but you can't stop us, even if you don't. Well, see ya 'round!' And he rolled off down the road.

'A cut in the deal'? If Torquil got *The Apple Star* into his grubby little hands, Lulu thought, it was very possible the le Bones would make lots of money out of it; but there was no way Torquil would be sharing any of it with Lulu. He was just trying to trick her into handing the book over. Ha! thought Lulu; as if any amount of money could persuade her to part with it anyway!

Lulu rubbed her arm, took a deep breath and walked on as nonchalantly as she could. Her face was burning; she hoped Torquil hadn't seen her blush. She replayed the whole scene in her mind, examining it for any telltale signs he might have picked up on; signs that she knew *exactly* what he was talking about.

Later that night, Lulu rang Cassandra but got no reply; she left a message.

Blue Corn

IMPORTANT

Love recipes must never be used frivolously. They are extremely complex; therefore, much can go wrong. The easiest recipes are those which have only a temporary effect; they are merely intended to put the eater in a romantic mood. But for such a momentous transformation as falling in love, a recipe has to work on many different levels. As Venus is the love planet, it is the plants she governs that we mostly turn to here. But those ruled by other planets come into play as well; the Sun's plants can help to influence the heart, as can those of Jupiter, with their happy aspect...even the plants of fiery Mars can help heat up the blood!

*

Lulu felt a tingle of anticipation as she read *The Apple Star*'s instructions at the beginning of the 'Matters of the Heart' section. She was excited now at the prospect of using it again. And she was fascinated; ever since she'd made the Truth Cookies, she'd been intrigued by the idea that every tree, flower and vegetable had a planetary influence. This book, by the mysterious Ambrosia May, had opened up a whole new world for her. Still, as she read on, she did feel a little nervous too.

> *You will need to perform some challenging rituals, with great care. You will need to know your two subjects' star signs, as the ingredients vary according to the twelve signs of the zodiac. You should consider the time of year; the best time for love recipes is fertile springtime, April-June, with May Eve and Midsummer the most potent times of all.*

That's good, thought Lulu. It was now May. She read further:

> *This section also includes recipes for falling out of love; particularly useful for undoing a love recipe which has gone wrong!*

It is important to note that certain foods should be avoided as much as possible by the two people you will be using the love recipe on, as they can have a negative effect on the potency of the love recipe. Dillweed, a Mercury plant, can get in the way of romance by shifting too much energy to the brain. Rational thought is the enemy of love! Jupiter-led lentils make one far too content to want to deal with the uncertainty of falling in love. And lettuce, governed by the Moon, is altogether too sleepy an influence. Therefore, these three – dillweed, lentils and lettuce – should be avoided at all costs.

Lulu cradled the book in her lap and thought for a moment. Dillweed, lentils and lettuce...she didn't think this would be a problem for Dad, but Jill was another matter; she wouldn't be surprised if Jill ate lentils and lettuce every day of the week. Lulu made a mental note to warn Frenchy.

Lulu began to flick through the actual recipes. There were different ones for different circumstances; recipes to use on people who had never met before; other recipes for proud, silent types who seemed incapable of loving anyone; and others for characters with extremely short attention spans, who couldn't focus on any one person long enough to fall in love with them. None of these fitted. Then Lulu turned the page and there it was:

Cupid Cakes

For those who have loved before, especially those who harbour lingering affection for an old love

Perfect! Lulu didn't know about Jill, but it was certainly true of Dad, perhaps in more ways than he ever let on. Part of him, Lulu knew, would always belong to Mum. It was right that it should, she thought, but not so much so that it kept him from getting on with life. Then again, knowing what he was like, Lulu couldn't be sure that a part of him wouldn't always belong to Varaminta, too. She began to read the recipe:

At least a week before you intend to use this recipe, you will need to obtain Dum'zani seeds. Plant them, and water them with your own tears. Because of the quantity of tears required, you may use onions to assist in generating them, and you may collect the tears in advance. However, you should spend at least one session weeping true tears of sorrow directly onto the seeds, as the tears of passion are the most fertile. Remember, 'They that sow in tears shall reap in joy'.

The Ðum'zani plant grows very rapidly – you need allow no more than a week's growth before proceeding with the recipe. When ready to harvest, the plant will have grown little blue cobs about four centimetres long, which resemble baby corn.

Good grief, thought Lulu. Ambrosia May was not kidding when she talked about 'challenging rituals'! Determined not to be discouraged, Lulu read on.

200g dolphin butter
3 doves' eggs
400g Łada flour
50ml almond-blossom honey
150g chopped dates

200g ground Ðum'zani corn, from self-seeded plants
pinch of powdered Ɓoyambe bark
24 drops Heartsease essence
1/4 teaspoon Myrrh
100ml cocoa-grape wine

Consult list below to determine the remaining ingredients, according to zodiac sign.

Lulu did so. The ingredient for Pisces, which was Dad's sign, was one teaspoon of grains of paradise, a diverting influence on the creative Piscean too busy to notice a potential love interest. She would have to find out what star sign Jill was later.

Lulu closed *The Apple Star* and thought about the recipe for a moment. Then she carefully put the precious, little yellow book away in its new hiding place; inside a cut-out section of an out-of-date encyclopedia. The encyclopedia was due for retirement anyway, since she had a newer one, but now she had found the perfect use for it. Lulu loved books, and her shelves were groaning with them, so when she put the encyclopedia back on the shelf she congratulated herself on how brilliantly concealed *The Apple Star* was.

Now she had a list of ingredients, Lulu needed to get hold of Cassandra even more urgently. She realised she still hadn't heard from her, so she tried calling again. Once again, she got the voicemail message: a brief instruction which didn't mention Cassandra by name. Lulu hung up without saying anything. She sighed and reached for the Mum-in-Muddy-Wellies photo beside her bed. 'Where *has* she got to?' Lulu wondered aloud. Not only did she need those ingredients, but she still hadn't been able to talk to

Cassandra about Varaminta's veiled threats – or her encounter with Torquil, for that matter. And Lulu did so want advice and reassurance from Cassandra, whose mystical understanding of the world was so different from anyone else's, yet made so much sense to Lulu.

As she thought about it, she realised Cassandra herself needed warning; for all Lulu knew, they might find out about her through her connection to Lulu and *The Apple Star*, and track her down too. Good grief, thought Lulu – what if they had already done so? What if something awful had happened to Cassandra, and that was why Lulu hadn't been able to get hold of her?

Tea and Cake

'I'll follow you, I'll lead you about a round,

  'Sometimes a horse I'll be, sometimes a hound...'

So said William, the boy who was playing Puck in the school play. The naughty little sprite was tormenting poor Bottom the weaver, whose head Puck had just transformed into that of an ass. Lulu shivered; the tormentor reminded her of Torquil – who, indeed, she and Frenchy had nicknamed the Torment – and she had the unshakeable sensation that she would encounter him again before long. And what sort of menace would he be if, like Puck, he could make such malicious magic at the expense of others?

'Psst, Lu!' whispered Frenchy. 'We're on in a minute – better go backstage.'

'Oh, OK.'

'Got your clothes for tonight?'

'Uh-huh.' Lulu was going to Frenchy's for supper, and after that Jill was taking them to the art gallery for the opening of Frenchy's dad's one-man show. Lulu's dad was due to meet them at the gallery straight from work.

'And guess who else is coming,' said Frenchy.

'Not the dreaded Basil Larsenbarsen?' said Lulu.

'Yup. Look,' said Frenchy, taking Lulu by the arm as they walked. 'When are we going to get your dad and my mum together for this famous tea and cake?'

Lulu groaned. 'Oh, I still can't get hold of Cassandra. I've tried a gazillion times. No word for a whole week. I hope she's OK.'

'Oh boy,' sighed Frenchy. 'Well, I'm sure she's just on holiday or something. You will keep trying though, won't you?'

'Yeah, of course,' said Lulu, as they made their way through to the wings. 'Oh, by the way, what's your mum's star sign?'

'Virgo. Why d'you ask?'

'I need to know, just in case,' said Lulu, leaning forward to whisper, ''cos the ingredients depend on it.'

Frenchy shook her head. 'Amazing. Oh hey, check this out,' she added mischievously, her attention suddenly diverted. 'Watch.'

On stage lay Glynnie Gudvitsa, languid and lovely, propped up on a pile of cushions. A lock of glossy blue-black hair fell artlessly across her face as she raised her head and stretched out her dark, slender arms. Jake Hershey stood nearby, supposedly engaged in scenery-painting but, in fact, more than a little bit distracted by Glynnie. He peered surreptitiously at her, his face half hidden by the collar of his shirt, which he always wore cocked at a jaunty angle.

Glynnie opened her liquid black eyes. 'What angel wakes me from my flowery bed?'

Jake Hershey shifted his gaze abruptly; his role in life was to be the subject of others' adoration, not to be seen adoring one who apparently didn't notice him. Frenchy dug Lulu in the ribs, suppressing a giggle.

Loitering close to Jake were Zena Lemon and Chantrelle Portobello. Like Jake, they had considered themselves too cool to be involved in the play. In truth, what they all had in common was laziness. But what none of them had realised was that Mr Drinkmoore was especially intent on engaging the workshy in the production – one way or another. It was now half-term week, and as he knew they were often up to no good when school was out, he saw this as the perfect opportunity for a full week of drama, crammed with rehearsals and production work. So Jake had a brush and a paintpot, and Zena and Chantrelle were to exercise their considerable bulk as scene-shifters. Zena had moaned about this, until she realised that it meant she got to hang around close to Jake. And 'close' was definitely on the agenda, as far as Zena was concerned; unlike Jake, Zena didn't care who knew if she had a soft spot for someone. Far from it.

'There's your reason Zena hates Glynnie,' whispered Frenchy, as they watched Zena trying in vain to divert Jake's attention from his painting.

'You bet,' agreed Lulu. She watched as Glynnie-as-Titania declared her loving devotion for the grotesque Bottom. A disaster brought about by mischievous fairies – yet, thought Lulu, wasn't love disastrous enough without such interference? Zena loves Jake, but Jake loves Glynnie; and Glynnie doesn't care. Dad had loved Varaminta, a disaster by any measure. Jill did love Jack, Frenchy's dad, once, but now she loved the pompous Basil Larsenbarsen – apparently. All making asses of themselves. Oh, why did the whole business have to be so complicated? All the more reason, Lulu supposed, to try and help; unlike the naughty Puck she would be like a *good* fairy, bringing order to it all, instead of more mess.

Marzipan Man

'I don't get it. What's it supposed to be?' asked Lulu. She and Frenchy were standing in front of a large painting by Jack Fry, Frenchy's dad.

Frenchy read the label. 'It's called *Kindhearted Woman Blues*.'

'Can't make out a woman at all,' Lulu said, squinting. 'And where's the blue?'

'No,' explained Frenchy, 'it's a picture of a *song* called "Kindhearted Woman Blues".'

'How can you paint a song?' said Lulu.

'That's how Dad works,' said Frenchy. 'He listens to CDs and just paints the images in his head.'

'That's right,' said Frenchy's dad, appearing beside Lulu. 'See, it's not about the words of the song, but the shapes and colours the music suggests to me.'

Lulu stared at the picture, trying to figure out what sounds it would make, if it were music.

'Hey, girls!' said Lulu's dad, who had just arrived.

'Dad!' Lulu gave him a hug.

'Hi, I'm Jack,' said Frenchy's dad. The two fathers shook hands.

'I'm Mike; pleased to meet you,' said Lulu's dad. 'Great paintings! That's interesting, what you were just saying, about the music. So the blues aren't blue?'

Jack smiled. 'Not to me, but, y'know, everyone's different.' He looked at the painting and shook his head. 'Cor, but I was hurting when I painted that!' He took Mike's arm. 'Got some more upbeat ones over here. You like jazz, bebop?'

'I love it!' said Mike, and the two of them moved away.

'Well, they've certainly hit it off,' observed Frenchy.

'Yeah. Wrong parent though,' said Lulu, casting her eyes around the room for Jill. She eventually caught sight of her nodding slowly as she listened to Basil Larsenbarsen expounding fulsomely – about his magnum opus, no doubt. 'How can she prefer *him* to your dad?'

'Oh, it's complicated,' said Frenchy. 'Mum says Dad's really hard to live with. For ages, people weren't buying his paintings. He had to borrow money, he got really depressed about it and... Oh my—' Frenchy's face turned white, her eyes staring past Lulu. 'You won't *believe* who just walked in!'

'Who?' said Lulu, turning to look. And there, blowing air-kisses in all directions, shiny-shouldered in a loud black-and-white dress that dazzled the eye, was...Varaminta le Bone. Her beady-eyed Poochie poked its black-and-white be-ribboned head out of a similarly patterned dog carrier under her arm.

Lulu's jaw fell open. 'What the heck is she doing here?'

'Well, she *could* have been invited,' ventured Frenchy. 'She might have seen Dad's work and wanted to buy—'

'Rubbish!' interrupted Lulu. 'I'm sure she's got someone spying on me; that weirdo with the beard at the gallery, I bet... She's probably been tracking Dad, too. She knew we'd be here, all right, and she's up to something, I swear. The question is, what?'

'I admit, it does look that way,' said Frenchy. 'We know she's after, ahem, the book...' Frenchy's voice lowered to a whisper at the mention of Lulu's prize possession, 'but how is showing up here going to help her get it?'

They watched as Varaminta wafted over to Lulu's dad. 'She's got a flaming nerve!' gasped Lulu.

'Very clever,' said Frenchy. 'Nab him in public...even better, at a party. Where he won't just tell her where to get off in no uncertain terms...oh man!

Do you *see* the look on his face?'

Just as Varaminta approached Lulu's dad, the gallery owner tapped Jack on the shoulder and led him away to introduce him to someone. Lulu's dad was left alone with Varaminta.

Lulu felt a chill wave of dread. 'Oh my God, she's going to tell him about the book!'

'I wouldn't be so sure...' said Frenchy. 'I think she'll have to be a bit craftier than that if she wants to get her hands on it.'

Just then, Frenchy's dad appeared beside them. 'Ah, there you are, Mandy love. Your Aunt Karen and co. have just arrived, they're dying to see you. Come on, over here! You too, Lulu.'

'Oh, er...well, I um—'

'Lulu's got someone else to see,' said Frenchy quickly, 'but I'll be right there, Dad – just give me a minute, OK?'

Jack gave her the thumbs up. 'Over there, by the drinks. See you!'

'Listen, I'd better join them,' said Frenchy, when he had gone. 'But you go and spy on Varaminta. I'll get away when I can, all right?'

Lulu gazed across the crowd, trying to find Varaminta again after the distraction. 'OK,' she said vaguely as she set off. 'I'll see you later, then.'

Frenchy patted her on the shoulder and headed off in the other direction.

The room was more crowded now, but even with Varaminta in her dazzling dress Lulu couldn't see her or Dad anywhere. Panic began to clutch at her throat; where could they be? The gallery was up one flight of stairs in an old warehouse building, and now Lulu threw herself out into the bleak, industrial hallway: it was deserted. At the end of the hall was a huge freight lift, empty but for a greasy-looking boy slumped in a seat in the corner, reading an action-hero comic. He lowered the comic and observed her coolly. 'Looking for someone?' he asked.

'Um. Did a man and woman come this way?'

'Black-and-white dress?'

'Yes!'

'Oh, yeah,' said the boy. 'Took 'em upstairs. Gallery's on two floors, you know. Did you want to go up?'

'Uh...I suppose so, yes please.'

Lulu stepped into the iron cage of a lift, the most old-fashioned she had ever seen. The entrance to the floor had to be opened and closed by hand, as did the heavy iron latticed gate that the boy now slid shut with a loud clunk. He pushed a lever, and the cage began to grind and rattle its way northwards through naked layers of concrete and steel. Lulu suddenly felt trapped; something didn't feel right about this. If the gallery has two floors, she thought, how come no one else is going in and out? The boy smirked greasily at her, and she shifted her gaze, staring resolutely at the floor. After what felt like an age, the lift squealed to a halt, and the boy slid the gate open.

'Uh, thank you,' said Lulu, and she stepped out hesitantly into another deserted hallway. She turned around quickly. 'Will you wait for...' she began, but the door shut in her face, and she heard the *clunk!* of the gate behind it, then the grinding of the descending lift. She was alone. This definitely didn't feel right. 'Dad?' she called, her voice echoing around the dank walls. She stepped forward. 'Dad, it's me, Lulu!' she cried. 'Are you there?' Her voice trailed away into a squeak. She quickened her step, and searched for anything that looked like an entrance to another part of the gallery. But of the three doors that led off the passageway, none would open.

Lulu began to feel sick. 'Help!' she cried. She ran back to the lift door and banged on it. 'Let me out!' Nothing. She heard a whimper, then realised it had come from her. She leaned against the wall and put her face in her hands.

'Want me to get him back for you?' said a voice.

Lulu knew the voice instantly. She looked up. 'You...can't scare...me, Torquil,' she mustered, rather unconvincingly.

Torquil emerged from his hiding place, a little nook beside the lift chamber. He stepped forward, waving his mobile phone. 'Ha ha. I can get him for you, you know; all I have to do is text him, and he'll be right up.' He slipped the phone into his pocket. 'But not before we settle our little agreement! Remember?'

'*AAARRRGH!*' screamed Lulu, as loudly as she could, hoping someone below might hear.

'Sshh!' hissed Torquil, clamping a hand over her mouth. 'You're running out of time, Poodle,' he warned. Lulu shuddered at the sound of the old nickname Torquil used to torment her with constantly. 'You're gonna miss your chance to help us out here, get your cut in the deal, you know that? Ha! Pretty soon your dad's going to be like marzipan in my mum's hands again anyway...'

Lulu struggled, and pulled at his arm. Torquil tightened his grip. 'Oh, he won't admit it to *you*, of course,' he went on, 'but she's working her magic on him right now, as we speak.'

Lulu began to wriggle vigorously. So that was why Varaminta had shown up tonight. This was a two-pronged attack; while Torquil worked on Lulu,

Varaminta was sticking her claws into Dad, and it was all about getting hold of Lulu's wonderful book.

'All right, all right, keep your hair on!' said Torquil, as Lulu kicked out again. 'I'll text him now if you promise to keep quiet.' He let go of her slowly. Lulu gasped for air, and watched as he hit a few buttons on his phone. Seconds later, she was overjoyed to hear the clanking of the returning lift.

'Remember,' said Torquil, 'either you let us have that book, or my mum will just have to make your dad get it for her.' The lift ground to a halt on the other side of the door, and the gate slid open. Torquil let go of Lulu and opened the door. 'She always gets men to do what she wants, you know. Never fails.' Lulu stepped into the lift, turned and glowered at him.

'*Never!*' he added, before shutting the door.

Candy-Coated Anti-dote

'Where were you?' demanded Dad, as they descended into the street. 'I was looking for you all over!'

'I was looking for you!' squealed Lulu. 'You were with *her*, how could you! Where did you get to?'

'I was trying to get rid of her!' bellowed Dad, red-faced. 'I took her out here to put her in a cab.' Lulu was embarrassed that this perfectly logical explanation had escaped her. Dad slapped his head. 'Jeez, that woman!' He began marching ahead in great lolloping strides.

Lulu trotted along, trying to keep pace with him. 'What did she want?'

Dad didn't seem to hear. 'She's ruined my evening, that's for sure. Taxi!' he called out, as one appeared around the corner.

*

Lulu lay in bed, staring out of her skylight at the Truth Star. *She's working her magic on him... She always gets men to do what she wants, you know...*Torquil's words taunted her. Lulu hoped Torquil was wrong but as she pictured Dad's red face, she couldn't help wondering who he'd been angry at: Varaminta, for brazenly turning up like that, or himself because of the lingering emotions she'd roused in him, despite his assurances to Lulu to the contrary and all that Varaminta had done.

...He won't admit it to you, of course...

What *was* the truth?

Dad had calmed down in the cab home. But he'd started rattling on about Jack's art, the school play, English apples...anything but talk about what was really on his mind.

Bee-beep, bee-beep. Her phone! Someone was texting her very late. Lulu threw back the covers and turned on the light. She raced over to her dresser and grabbed the phone.

LOOK OUTSIDE. CASSANDRA X

At last! thought Lulu. She dashed to the window; out in the street stood a black cab. The headlights flashed twice. Lulu took *The Apple Star* from its new hiding place, went to the bedroom door and peeked into the hall; Dad's light was out. Lulu crept out of her room and down the stairs. Hurriedly, she slipped into her flip-flops and hoody and stepped out of the side door, taking care to leave it on the latch. The rear door of the cab swung open as Lulu reached the front garden, revealing a lit interior, complete with blue velvet seats, and Cassandra herself in the driving seat, glimpsed between blue curtains. Clutching the book, Lulu got into the back of the cab and closed its door. The interior plunged into darkness. 'Cassandra?'

'Hello, Lulu,' said Cassandra from the front, her face dimly lit by a street lamp.

Lulu was reminded of the first time she met Cassandra; how she was spellbound by her big, dark eyes and rich, deep voice. At first, Lulu had found her overwhelming, even a little scary, with her billowing purple robe and the exotic whiff of magic that surrounded her. But seeing her now felt like coming home; comforting, reassuring. Lulu leaned forward, resting her hand on the frame of the window that separated them. 'Oh, Cassandra, where on earth have you been?' she asked in a loud whisper.

'Cairo,' said Cassandra. 'I spend quite a lot of time there, I'm afraid. I'm sorry I wasn't here when you needed me. You're worried about something; what is it?'

Lulu heaved a sigh of relief. 'Oh, I'm so glad you're OK! I didn't know what to think, anything could've...' She took a deep breath and started at the beginning, explaining all about Varaminta's interview in *Chow!* magazine, the visit from the movers, Varaminta's appearance at the gallery, and her own encounters with Torquil. 'And I think Grodmila's still working for Varaminta,' she went on, adding sheepishly, 'she saw the Truth Cookies when I baked them, and she might have seen *The Apple Star* at the same time.' Lulu felt embarrassed that she hadn't been more careful with the book around Grodmila.

'So you're worried they'll steal it,' said Cassandra.

'Yes! Maybe not Varaminta herself, but someone working for her. It's too easy.' Lulu's voice grew more and more shrill as she went on. 'Those removals guys could have got a key...and Varaminta knows roughly when the house might be empty in the daytime, and Torquil—'

Cassandra laid her hand on top of Lulu's. 'Hush, no need to worry yourself so!' Lulu fell silent. 'You're right to be concerned about the book,' Cassandra went on. 'It must be kept out of the hands of people like Varaminta and her son at all costs. It was intended for you to use, only you, as you know, and from what I understand of those two...nasty, very nasty. But I have some special techniques for warding off intruders. So I can teach you what to do; it's simple really, just a bit of planting and sprinkling.'

'And they really work?'

'I've never been broken into yet. Security is about a good deal more than mere ironmongery. The important thing is to have *faith*, use the techniques with conviction. There's a saying: "If the Sun and Moon should doubt, they'd immediately go out..."' Cassandra paused, lost in thought, something she had a habit of doing.

'I'd never thought of it like that,' said Lulu, eventually.

'It's all about faith, my dear, therein lies the power,' said Cassandra, coming back down to Earth. 'Well now! I will send you everything in the post, along with instructions...no, we can do better than that. I remember noticing when I came here before that your house has a coal hole.'

'It does?' said Lulu.

'Yes, right near your front door. There's a round iron coal-hole cover; I noticed the design on it.'

'Oh, that thing. I didn't know it was for coal.'

'Yes; a hundred years ago, the coal man would open it up and pour the coal down a chute into the cellar, where it was stored. You might check that the cover will still come off. I could come along at night and slip in the things you need, carefully wrapped, of course. It will help if you place something soft, like a blanket, in the cellar beneath the chute. You know where I mean? You *can* get down there, I hope?'

'Oh, yes.'

'Good. This would be the safest way, I think. I promise to be discreet, and completely silent!'

'That would be brilliant, thank you! Um, Cassandra? Can I ask you something else?'

'Of course. What is it?'

'Well, it's just...there's another recipe I need to make.'

'Oh?'

'It's, er...Cupid Cakes.' Lulu was grateful for the darkness that hid her blush.

'May I see?'

Lulu handed Cassandra *The Apple Star*, open at the relevant page.

Cassandra turned on a dim yellow overhead light and read. 'Hmmm...oh! Ah-h-h...hmmm.'

Lulu fidgeted with her hoody zip.

'Hmmm,' said Cassandra again. At last, she peered at Lulu. 'I hope you realise how serious this is?'

'Yes, I—'

'"Not to be used for frivolous purposes"; you have read the introduction to this section, I hope?'

'Uh, yes.'

'Dum'zani seeds, eh?'

'Have you got those?' Lulu asked, unable to conceal her excitement.

Cassandra studied Lulu closely, saying nothing for a moment. 'I have,' she said at last. 'It's not for me to ask what you want this for. All I ask is that you sleep on it. This is another Level Three recipe, like the Truth Cookies you made. The most powerful of all; it's important that you understand the consequences of using it. Search your conscience, Lulu. If you truly believe this is the right thing to do, then I will help you. That is one condition. The other is that you make the Candy-Coated Anti-Dote at the same time. These things can go wrong, you know. But at least if you have the Anti-Dote, you can reverse the effect of the Cupid Cakes immediately, and no damage will be done.'

'Oh, definitely, I promise,' Lulu assured her.

'Sleep on it, Lulu,' said Cassandra again. 'Meanwhile, I will deliver the house-protection things tomorrow night. Make sure you have the cellar prepared. If there's any problem, call me.'

'Thank you,' said Lulu, opening the door.

'And Lulu,' said Cassandra.

'Yes?'

'Remember, be calm and confident. You have nothing to fear but fear itself.'

Pepperland

Lulu slept on it. She spent quite a lot of time lying awake on it, too, staring at the night sky. She read her horoscope:

> You're biding your time and crab-walking sideways – but try taking a step forward, and you might just surprise yourself!!

Lulu sighed and dropped the magazine on the floor. She shut her eyes, but the image of Varaminta in her black-and-white dress kept coming back, and the way she had looked at Dad, gently touching his arm. Lulu shuddered. 'But I *trust* Dad,' she reminded herself, as she gazed at the Truth Star. 'I mean, there's no way he could fall for her again, after everything he's learned about her...is there?'

The star twinkled, and the words popped into Lulu's head, 'Believe in him.'

Yes, Lulu told herself, so I should. It ought to have made her feel better about things, but instead her mind filled with doubt. The words, 'believe in him' suddenly reminded her of a young office assistant Dad had once hired, who had a criminal record. 'The kid's got to start somewhere,' Dad had said. He was sure that the lad really meant to turn over a new leaf, and he had been right; three years later, the young man was still a loyal and popular employee, never once getting into trouble. 'All he needed was for someone to believe in him,' Dad had said.

What if Varaminta were to take advantage of Dad's good nature, convincing him that she, too, was a reformed character? And if he fell for her again, not only would it be disastrous for him, he might, without knowing what he did, help Varaminta and Torquil get to *The Apple Star*, by letting them in. It was one thing for Lulu to protect the book from intruders, but from invited guests...?

And then there was Basil Larsenbarsen. From Frenchy's bulletins, Jill's attachment to him appeared to be going from strength to strength. As Lulu drifted off to sleep, an image of him hovered in her mind's eye; the pallid face, the black-rimmed spectacles. Mister Black-and-White. What was it with all the black-and-white, she wondered drowsily. It was like Pepperland in the old Beatles film, *Yellow Submarine*. All joy had been squeezed out of Pepperland, until the heroes came along, bringing back colour and life, singing, 'All You Need is Love'...

When she woke up the next morning, Lulu realised she hadn't changed her mind about using the Cupid Cakes. The job she'd started with the Truth Cookies wasn't over yet; Dad was still at risk from Varaminta...and so was *The Apple Star*. She'd be helping Jill too, as well as Frenchy – and who would suffer? No one. If anything didn't go according to plan, it could all be undone by the Candy-Coated Anti-Dote anyway.

It was a no-brainer; she was determined to take that 'step forward' that her horoscope suggested and go through with it.

*

'What's with all the gardening all of a sudden?' said Aileen, grinning.

'I like it,' said Lulu simply, as she patted the moist earth where she had just planted her seeds. 'I like watching things grow. It's fun.' Naturally, she wasn't telling Aileen that she was in fact following Cassandra's instructions for protecting the house from intruders. Aileen would howl with laughter at such an idea anyway. As arranged, Cassandra had slipped a little package into the coal chute; it contained a packet of seeds, a small bottle encased in bubble wrap and written instructions. Everything had gone beautifully according to plan. Lulu was now in the front garden, working on number four out of the five plantings that she had to do. She had carefully plotted them, three in the back garden and two in the front, as evenly spaced as possible, picturing in her mind the points of a star as instructed. How she was going to explain the other part of the procedure, Lulu was less sure. The bottle was filled with a clear liquid, a herb-infused water, which was to be sprinkled at every doorway, window, fireplace and air vent throughout the house. She would have to be discreet.

'Yeah, you're right,' said Aileen, crouching nearby. 'It *is* fun; I've got some gorgeous new geraniums for my window box. What are you planting there, then?'

'Oh, it's...' Lulu realised she had no idea; there was nothing written on the bag they came in. 'Um, I can't actually remember.'

Aileen nudged her affectionately. 'You Poms, you're so daft! What does it say on the packet?' She reached for the crumpled brown paper bag that lay on the ground at Lulu's feet.

'Delphiniums!' Lulu blurted out quickly, saying the first thing that came into her head. 'That's right,' she said, beaming at Aileen. 'Delphiniums.'

'Well, that sounds nice,' said Aileen, straightening up. 'Oh, look who's here.'

Lulu looked up. Phil, Aileen's new boyfriend, had just parked his motorbike and was slowly lumbering towards them, jeans swishing. Assorted zips jangled and jingled against the squeaky black leather of his jacket. Phil was easily a foot taller than Aileen.

Aileen strained upwards and gave Phil a peck on the cheek. 'Hello, you,' she said.

'All right?' said Phil, winking at her.

'Hello, Phil,' said Lulu.

Phil nodded. 'All right?'

'Lulu's planting delphiniums,' said Aileen. 'Come inside. I've just got to finish making the supper.'

'All right,' said Phil. He gave Lulu one of his deadpan winks, brief as a butterfly's flutter, and swished, jangled and squeaked his way inside, behind Aileen. Lulu had already worked out that, what little language Phil used, he modulated in infinitely subtle ways to mean different things. The twinkling wink he'd given Aileen said, 'Hello, gorgeous, you're mine,' while the one he used for Lulu said, 'See ya 'round, kid.' Phil was nothing if not economical. Lulu tried to imagine the conversations he and Aileen had when they were alone together, but found it quite impossible. Perhaps they didn't get many chances for conversation anyway; apart from the day job as a fishmonger, Phil was a drummer in a fishmonger grunge band called Gutted. He and Aileen spent a great deal of time in very noisy places. They probably just smiled at each other a lot. Lulu hadn't made her mind up yet what kind of sweet Phil was; she wanted to like him, but found him hard to get to know. Perhaps he was a Kiddie Egg; one of those little chocolate eggs with a toy inside. You might get something fun and interesting when you open it up...or else something incredibly boring that just sits in your jacket pocket for six months, accumulating fluff.

Lulu finished the planting and went inside, heading straight upstairs to her room. With Aileen distracted by Phil, and Dad not home yet, she decided it was a good time to do some sprinkling. She could do all the upstairs rooms now, leaving the downstairs for later that night, after Dad had gone to bed. She took the little bottle over to her bedroom window and unscrewed the cap. She paused, thinking: this feels daft! But then she remembered Cassandra's words, which stressed how important it was to believe in what she was doing. It wouldn't work, otherwise. Lulu thought of Cassandra's saying about the Sun and the Moon, and recalled her words from the very first time they had met, *never dismiss the symbolic... Have faith, my dear!* It was like learning to swim, Lulu decided. No matter how much teaching you had, it wasn't until you believed you could push yourself out into the water and not sink that you became a swimmer. Not a moment before.

Well, I did make the Truth Cookies work, Lulu told herself; I can do the same now. She shook the first droplets out onto the window ledge. As she moved from window to air vent to fireplace, and on to the next room, she pictured an invisible force field growing around the house, like a gigantic, luminous spider's web. Now, she thought, no le Bones or their (bearded) minions will be breaking in and getting their hands on *The Apple Star*. My magic will send them on their way.

After she had finished, Lulu phoned Cassandra and thanked her.

'And Cassandra? – I've decided to go ahead with the Cupid Cakes.'

Cassandra was silent for a moment. 'All right. You'd better read out those ingredients, then. *And* the ones for the Candy-Coated Anti-Dote.'

Lulu did so, remembering to include the grains of

paradise for her Pisces Dad, and the dried Osun plantain flakes which, with their Nigerian water-and-love goddess influence, were the ingredient for Earth-sign Virgos, like Jill, in need of romantic refreshment.

'Good,' said Cassandra. 'Now I have a note of these, I'll make sure I have them in stock. I'll deliver the Dum'zani seeds tonight, so you can get on with growing the plant, and the rest of the ingredients when you're ready for them.'

Lulu filled up with a wonderfully Christmas-Eve-ish feeling of anticipation. 'Thank you!' she said. 'Well, goodbye.' After putting the phone down, she remembered there was something important she had meant to tell Frenchy about the recipe. She consulted the 'Love Recipes' section again; oh yes, here it was: '...certain foods should be avoided...can have a negative effect on the potency of the love recipe...dillweed...lentils...lettuce.'

She *must* remember to tell Frenchy.

Lentils

'Oh man, why didn't you tell me before?' groaned Frenchy. It was Saturday afternoon, and they were sitting in Frenchy's bedroom, Lulu having scheduled an emergency meeting cunningly disguised as a dance practice session for the play.

'I'm sorry, I forgot. What with all that Torquil business and everything, it slipped my mind. And I had no idea where Cassandra was, or even if I'd ever see her again.'

Frenchy sighed. 'My mum grows lettuces on our allotment; we eat them all the time!'

'Oops! Oh well, you'll just have to make sure she doesn't have the other things from now on. I mean, as much as you can. And...I don't know, perhaps you can persuade her to make coleslaw instead of green salad? Say you fancy a change? You've got a bit of time, anyway. There's these seeds I have to plant, a kind of corn, and then I have to give the corn time to grow.'

'Oh boy, that'll take ages!'

'No, apparently it only takes a week. So if I plant the seeds this afternoon, that means I'll be able to harvest them next Saturday. Then I can make the Cupid Cakes that day, ready for tea next Sunday!'

Frenchy's eyes widened. 'They grow in one week? Whatever next – giant beanstalks?!'

'Well, it's true,' said Lulu. 'And that's not even the weirdest part. I have to cry onto them.'

'What?' Frenchy burst out laughing.

'Yeah, Cassandra explained it all to me. The idea is, the more sorrow you pour into them, the more joy the corn is packed with when you harvest it. It's a bit like a vaccine; you know, when you get injected with a little bit of a disease, and that makes your body develop the antibodies to that disease. Funnily enough, the cobs are blue, but they make you feel the opposite of blue. They make you feel super-happy, like you just want to hug everyone and tell them you love them.'

'But we don't want them to love *everyone*, just each other!'

Lulu put her hands on her hips. 'Yes, of course,' she said, 'that's why there's other ingredients, silly! And you'll never guess what; you know that "purple flower" in *A Midsummmer Night's Dream*? The one called Love-in-Idleness?'

'Yeah.'

'There really is such a flower.'

Frenchy cuffed Lulu on the arm. 'Ha – whaddaya know, I was right!'

'Yup,' acknowledged Lulu. 'It's called Heartsease, and it's the ingredient that makes you unable to take your eyes off someone. Then there's something called a cocoa grape; can you believe it, a grape that tastes of *chocolate*, and a special kind of wheat flour that you can only get from some Russian island associated with a Slavic love goddess, and dolphin butter—'

'*Dolphin* butter?!'

'I know, weird huh? Dolphins are associated with Aphrodite, the Greek goddess of love, because she was born from the foam of the sea. Then there's the special things you put in according to the people's signs of the zodiac.'

'Nothing out of the ordinary, then!' joked Frenchy.

Lulu laughed. 'The point is, when you love someone, it's a whole mish-mash of emotions. What the recipe does is to bring together a bunch of ingredients that give you those emotions. It's very scientific. Fifty percent joyfulness, thirty percent physical attraction—'

'Only thirty percent?'

'French, this is *love* we're talking about, not just fancying someone. And it's a different proportion for each love recipe. I picked Cupid Cakes because Dad's been in love before. So the cocoa grape, right, that part's for forgetting.'

'I was wondering,' said Frenchy. 'What if it went wrong somehow? Like, you know how in *A Midsummer Night's Dream*, there's that anti-dote?'

'Oh right, I meant to tell you. There's another recipe I'm making too; the Candy-Coated Anti-Dote. Geddit? Anti-*Dote*, to stop you *doting* on someone?'

Frenchy smiled. 'Oh, very good. Well then, we've got nothing to lose, have we?'

Then Jill called them for lunch.

Frenchy stood up. 'You are staying for lunch, right?'

Lulu's heart sank. 'Uh, yeah. Great.'

As the two of them headed towards the kitchen, Frenchy sniffed. 'Uh-oh.'

'Uh-oh what?' said Lulu.

'Smells like dal.' Frenchy sniffed some more.

'What's dal?' Lulu asked, sniffing too.

Frenchy sighed. 'Lentils.'

Rats, thought Lulu.

Worse still, they found Basil Larsenbarsen sitting at the kitchen table.

'Well, helleauo!' he said. 'It's Lulu, am Oi roight?'

'Yu-huh,' said Lulu vaguely, more concerned with what was bubbling in the pot on the stove. Frenchy looked worried, too; she went over and lifted the pot lid.

Behind her mum's back, she nodded gravely to Lulu. Jill busied herself with laying the table, and Lulu offered a hand. She glanced back at Frenchy, who had taken out a jar of hot chilli peppers and was now loosening its perforated cover.

'Oops!' cried Frenchy, as the entire contents of the chilli jar fell into the lentils. Lulu smacked a hand to her mouth, supposedly in surprise, but really to conceal a mischievous smirk.

'Oh, *Amanda*!' cried Jill.

'I'm sorry, it just fell off,' said Frenchy. 'Well, I guess the dal's history, never mind, I'm happy with a sandwich.'

'Eao, nonsense, it's easily rectifiable,' insisted Basil Larsenbarsen, getting up. 'All you need is a potato and lots of lemon juice; you won't know the difference.' He took a spoon and scooped out what he could of the chilli peppers.

Frenchy rolled her eyes at Lulu.

But Jill smiled affectionately at Basil. Then she opened the fridge door. 'It so happens I've got some leftover mashed potato!' She pulled out a bowl of white stuff that was going grey around the edges. Lulu grimaced.

'Perfect!' said Basil.

Jill leaned into the fridge again. 'And look, here's a lemon!' she announced happily.

Although Lulu and Frenchy still found the resulting

concoction too spicy, Jill and Basil, to the girls' dismay, soldiered on, determined to enjoy their dal.

'So Lulu, are you a *femme fata-a-ahl*, loik the girl in the play?' Basil asked suddenly.

Lulu lowered her cheese sandwich and squinted at him. 'Am I *what*? What play?'

'Baz, really!' laughed Jill. 'Don't take any notice of him, Lulu; there's a play called *Lulu* but Baz is just teasing you.'

Basil's shoulders went up and down as he did a sort of smirky, closed-mouthed chuckle. 'Hm-hm-hm!' he went. Lulu smouldered at him.

'*I* know what that means,' said Frenchy, crossly. 'And no, she's not! Lu, he's asking if you're dangerous to men. It's French.'

'Oh, Mandy, it was only a joke, darling,' said Jill.

'Well, *I* don't think it's very funny.'

'Ah,' mumured Basil, apparently revelling in his annoying-ness, 'but as we all *kneaow*, the female of the species *is* more deadly than the male.' Then he was explaining at great length why this was just as true of humans as it was in the animal kingdom, giving a detailed description of his zoological research for his magnum opus.

'So you see,' he said finally, as Lulu was edging her way out of the kitchen, 'whether it's Eve in the Gordon of Eden, or Pandora opening that box of demons, it's *females* who are the source of all trouble!'

'Oh, Baz!' chuckled Jill, shoving him affectionately. 'You're such a tease!'

*

They sat eating apples in Frenchy's room afterwards. 'Sorry about the dal,' said Frenchy.

'It's OK, you tried,' said Lulu, examining the five-pointed star shape the seeds in her apple made. Ever since reading about the two 'apple stars' that always showed themselves if you sliced across the middle, she never could resist cutting an apple this way before eating it. 'Hey, you got a bible handy?'

'Er, why?'

'I want to check the beginning bit...Genesis,' said Lulu. 'See, I remember there was an Eve and an Adam, but I don't remember it mentioning any *Gordon*.'

'Pff-ff-ff!' went Frenchy, laughing uncontrollably and spitting bits of apple everywhere. 'That was – that was the *snake's* name!' she managed to say, before rolling onto her side in fits of laughter. This set Lulu off, too. Tears rolled down Frenchy's cheeks, but a moment later they turned into tears of sorrow, together with real sobs.

'Oh French!' said Lulu, sitting up. 'Hey, are

you all right?'

Frenchy pulled a tissue from a box beside the bed, and blew her nose. 'Oh, I'm sorry. It's just...oh!' She sniffed and toyed with the tissue. Lulu put her arm around her.

'He's so...creepy,' said Frenchy. 'Plus, he only ever talks about himself, have you noticed? He's so full of himself!'

Lulu frowned. 'He is odd – all that stuff about women being trouble... We've got to think of a reason for asking your mum to tea *alone*,' said Lulu. 'Otherwise she might invite him along. Hmmm.'

They sat in silence for a moment. Lulu twiddled her apple stalk between her fingers. Then she had an idea. 'I know – apples!'

'Huh?'

'OK, your mum's a teacher, right?'

'Yeah.'

'And a gardener too. Well, Dad's got this new client, the English Apple Marketing Board. They're inventing characters based on the different kinds of apple. We could tell her he needs her as an advisor!'

Frenchy slapped her on the back. 'Brilliant! And you tell your dad that Mum's dead clever, and really into fruit and stuff – which she is – and knows all about how to get kids interested!'

'Deal!' said Lulu.

Strong Onions

Think about Varaminta, Lulu told herself. No, that didn't work – it brought teeth-grinding anger, but no tears. OK, think about Mum; think about how it felt when Torquil took your pictures of her. No use; only more anger...

Lulu sat back on her heels and sighed. This was proving harder than she'd imagined. I must be a rubbish actor, she thought. Good actors could cry at the drop of a hat. She was in the back garden, and had just planted her Dum'zani seeds. She'd even managed – secretly, in her bedroom – to collect some tears in a cup, but then there had been onions involved. Even using super-strong, fresh, yellow onions, Lulu had been disappointed at how little liquid her tears had amounted to; probably only a quarter of a cup, and a very small coffee cup at that. It had been tricky too! She'd wasted a lot of tears simply by not catching them before they fell on the floor and seeped into the carpet.

Dad waved to her from the window; Lulu waved back, hoping to convey a casual everything's-going-fine-I-don't-need-any-help look. That was part of the problem, she realised; she was out in the garden, not safely tucked away in the seclusion of her room, where no one was likely to bother her. Their neighbour, Ian Cakebread, might pop his head over the garden fence at any moment. Dad might decide to come out and read his paper. It was all very distracting.

She had to lose herself in her imagination, Lulu decided, and whenever she needed to do this, she turned to books and films. She needed a sad story, and now she remembered, from years ago, *Bambi*. It was when she was in reception class; all her friends had seen it, but she hadn't been allowed. Dad had thought Lulu would find it too upsetting, because of what happened in it. But then she saw it at a friend's house, anyway... And now Lulu pictured Bambi coming out of the cave, calling for his mother. A lump came to Lulu's throat as she thought about it, and she leaned over the patch of earth where she'd planted the seeds.

"*Mother? Mother!*" the little deer had cried, his long-lashed eyes searching.

Oh! Poor Bambi – the tears started flowing – Mother's *dead*!

Lulu was completely unaware of how loudly she

was sobbing, until she heard Ian Cakebread's voice saying, 'Lulu, are you all right?'

Lulu fell silent, still staring at the moist brown earth beneath her. She watched a tear slide to the end of her nose and drip – *plop!* – onto the ground, as she thought about what to say. Then she wiped her face with her sleeve, and looked up. 'Oh, it's nothing really,' she said brightly. 'Just a dead mouse.' She sniffed loudly. 'Silly me!'

Ian Cakebread, who was holding his beloved Siamese cat, Sushi, peered over the fence. 'Oh, were you burying it?'

'Er – yes! That's right. It's in the ground now. Uh-huh.'

Sushi leapt from her owner's arms onto the grass beside Lulu. 'Oh, Soosh!' Ian reprimanded the cat.

Sushi began pawing at the freshly-dug earth where the Dum'zani seeds were planted. 'Oh, no no no!' said Lulu, picking her up.

'Come on, Soosh!' said Ian, stretching out his arms to take the cat back. 'Better put a heavy gravestone over that mouse, if you don't want this one getting at it!' he said, as he walked back towards his house.

In fact, it had looked very much to Lulu as if Sushi had been about to relieve herself, and now Lulu began to worry if cat's wee would ruin the magic. Short of putting up a notice saying 'CATS – KEEP OFF!' she couldn't immediately think what she could do. Then there was the gardener to think of. Because Dad never found time to do any gardening himself, old Costas the Greek gardener came in once a week; she'd have to tell him what not to dig up. Perhaps he'd have some advice about cat's wee, too.

*

Lulu woke early the next morning, brimming over with nervous anticipation. She had to go and look right away; see if it was really working. If it was – if her tears had done the trick – the Dum'zani plant could grow as much as two metres in just six days. So something ought to be showing right away. Lulu crept past Dad's room – he was still snoring away – down the stairs, and out the back door.

Flap flap flap went the crows that had collected on the lawn, as they flew away. And there it was; her plant, in all its glory. Right in the centre of the little anti-cat-toilet fortress Lulu had hastily built around it (rocks, and a high circle of canes) stood a tall, bright green shoot. Hugging herself for warmth in the chill morning air, she moved towards it, the dewy grass cold on her flip-flopped feet. She gazed at it in wonder, for already it came up as far as her knees, and a few leaves were beginning to form along the sides. 'Hello,' Lulu whispered.

*

'I told Dad about next Sunday,' Lulu told Frenchy on Monday morning. 'And guess what, he thinks it's a brilliant idea.'

'Mum's cool with it too—' said Frenchy.

'Great!'

'Only trouble is, we're away next weekend.'

'Oh, rats!' said Lulu, deflated. 'But we're doing the play the following weekend, both days.'

'I know...'

'And then Dad's away the weekend after that!'

Frenchy winced. 'Eek. This isn't great.'

'I mean, really, French, we can't afford to leave this too late; there's no telling *what* Varaminta will do to get hold of the book before then. And the recipe works best at this specific time of year, and—'

At that moment, Miss Broccoli entered the room. 'Good morning, everyone!' she called out. There was much shuffling, chatting, unpacking of books, during which Miss Broccoli tried desperately to establish enough hush to take the register.

Glynnie Gudvitsa, who sat next to Lulu, on the other side from Frenchy, took a small black box from her backpack, opened it and removed a pair of spectacles. She put them on and sat, chin up, staring straight ahead.

'Hey, are those new?' whispered Lulu.

Glynnie turned and grimaced. 'Yeah.'

'Join the club!' said Frenchy jovially, wiggling her own glasses at her.

Glynnie smiled wanly. 'Uh-huh...oh, here we go!' She rolled her eyes, as the rest of the class began to look at her. Zena made an ugly chortling-grunting noise like a warthog. She sneered and whispered to Chantrelle Portobello, whose lip curled smugly as she stared at Glynnie.

Miss Broccoli, noticing this, attempted in her well-intentioned yet doomed way to defend Glynnie. 'Those are nice spectacles, Galinda!' she pronounced gaily.

Glynnie chewed the inside of her lip in embarrassment. 'Thank you, Miss Broccoli,' she said quietly. 'It's just...for the board and stuff...' Her voice trailed off as her gaze shifted to the floor in front of her.

'Ah, lucky for you, then,' Miss Broccoli went on blithely, 'you won't be needing them for your acting!'

Oh, stop going on about it, thought Lulu, feeling

Glynnie's skin-crawling resentment.

'No, that's right,' said Glynnie, as she slid down in her seat.

'Oh, wot a shame,' said Zena Lemon, 'we wanted a four-eyed fairy queen, ditn't we?' Chantrelle and the rest of the gang murmured in agreement.

'All right, all right, enough of that,' said Miss Broccoli.

Jake Hershey, who sat in front of Zena, turned around and smouldered at her from behind his jaunty collar. 'Oh, you're *so* witty. Not.'

Zena took any communication from Jake as encouragement, no matter how hostile the intent. She leaned forward flirtatiously. 'At least *I* can see wot's in front of me, babe,' she purred. 'And I like it!'

Miss Broccoli banged on her desk with her ruler. 'The register!' she cried, and began calling out names.

Chinese Honey

Lulu was beginning to wonder when they would ever get Dad and Jill together until, on Wednesday, Frenchy had the best piece of news either of them could have hoped for. 'You'll never guess what,' she garbled excitedly, 'the friends we were going to visit this weekend got their plans mixed up...so we're not going away after all!'

'Yesss!' cried Lulu. 'So now all I have to do is get the rest of the ingredients from Cassandra.'

'And the ones for the Anti-Dote.'

'Oh, yeah, of course.'

By lunchtime, however, Lulu had begun to worry again, only this time it wasn't about the matchmaking tea.

'I've got to go to my piano lesson today,' she murmured grimly, picking at her sandwich. 'There's no getting out of it, and I bet Torquil will be lurking there, ready to pounce. Or else there'll be some other

Varaminta henchman, like that spooky man from the gallery, waiting to kidnap and take me to her or something. Oh, French!'

'Listen, I'll walk with you, OK?' said Frenchy, finishing off her hummus and gritty carrot.

Lulu's face unknotted itself. 'What, all the way? Are you sure?'

Frenchy straightened her glasses. 'Of course! It's not far – I'll just get the later bus, it's no biggie. I promised I'd help where I could, didn't I?'

'Oh, *thanks,* French!'

Frenchy looked at her watch. 'Come on,' she said, 'let's get over to the rehearsal.'

On stage, two girls were having a great time pretending to fight. 'I am not yet so low,' snarled the smaller one, 'but that my nails can reach unto thine *eyes*!' She lunged at the other in mock anger, hands mimicking claws, and grinning like a Cheshire cat.

'Oh, come *on*,' interrupted Mr Drinkmoore, his eyes drooping wearily. 'She's just nicked your boyfriend, for heaven's sake! I want *seething hatred*, not two mates having a laugh!'

The two girls collapsed into giggles. 'Sorry!' they squealed.

This set off a few of the others as well, including Lulu and Frenchy.

'Quiet!' commanded Mr Drinkmoore, so forcefully that there was instant hush. He massaged the inner recesses of his eye sockets. 'Look, we've got ten days left to get this right. There's nothing more boring for an audience – even an audience of adoring mums and dads – than a poorly rehearsed play. You lot –' he indicated Lulu and Frenchy and several other spare parts '– you're not needed right now, so come back in twenty minutes. Off you go!'

On their way out, Lulu and Frenchy passed through a rather crowded lobby. There was Glynnie, desperately trying to get her fairy king's performance up to scratch. Jake Hershey stood on a flattened cardboard box nearby, painting a free-standing tree. He was assisted by Zena Lemon, who had foisted herself upon him, unasked.

All of a sudden Glynnie, who was not wearing her glasses, tripped on the triangular plywood support at the back of the tree and lunged forward, trying to regain her balance. Jake, who had been gazing at Glynnie's face as she passed, had also failed to notice where she was putting her feet, and now the tree threatened to topple over. He grabbed hold of it, but too late; the tree was stuck tight with paint to the cardboard underneath, so as the tree tipped sideways, so did the cardboard, dislodging Zena. Lulu and

Frenchy looked on aghast as Zena, who could easily have regained her footing if she'd tried, deliberately fell forward, knocking Jake over and flattening him.

'Get urff me!' came Jake's muffled protests from underneath Zena. Frenchy rushed over to right a pot of green paint that had fallen on its side, just in time to prevent it seeping all over Jake's hair. Reluctantly, Zena began to shift onto her knees, allowing Jake to breathe again.

Glynnie had scratched herself on the plywood and was inspecting her shin. Lulu went over to her. 'Are you all right?' she asked.

Glynnie was flushed with embarrassment. 'I'm OK, thanks; it's not really bleeding.' She gave a nervous giggle, as she glanced in Zena and Jake's direction. 'Think *he's* the one you want to worry about!' Then she turned away and bit her lip. 'I lied,' she confessed softly. 'About the glasses. I need them for a lot more than just the board. I hardly saw that thing in front of me just now.'

'Oh, never mind,' said Lulu, patting Glynnie's arm.

There was still quite a commotion behind them, among Jake and Zena's crowd. Drowned out by the noise, Glynnie went on, 'I *can't* play the part in glasses! It'll look ridiculous!'

'Can't you wear contact lenses?' said Lulu.

Glynnie shook her head. 'My parents can't afford them.'

'Then eat lots of carrots!' said Lulu.

'Get out of here, you don't believe that – do you?' said Glynnie, chuckling.

'No, it's true, honest!' insisted Lulu. '*Believe* me. I know what I'm talking about.'

Glynnie blinked at her, a little surprised at the strength of Lulu's conviction. 'OK...can't hurt, I guess...'

*

There was no sign of Torquil that afternoon when Lulu, accompanied by Frenchy, went to her piano lesson. No spooky man, either, for that matter. And Aileen picked her up straight from the teacher's house, so she got home without any problems, too.

That was all right, then.

Or was it? That evening, Lulu couldn't help wondering. Torquil might have been there, but avoided her when he saw she wasn't alone – that had been the idea, of course. But Lulu hadn't been prepared for the creeping doubt that was now invading her thoughts: perhaps he and Varaminta had just changed tactics. Perhaps they'd given up on the threats, and had decided to bypass her altogether, as promised.

'But there's no way Varaminta or Torquil could get the book themselves, is there?' Lulu said to Mum-in-Muddy-Wellies. Mum smiled back at her, reminding Lulu of the sprinkled herb water and her little protective flowers that were now showing in the garden. ('Not like any delphiniums I've ever seen,' Aileen had remarked, puzzled, as she'd inspected the small pink blooms with star-shaped stamens.)

No, Lulu was convinced she could ward off intruders successfully...but maybe Torquil had given up on persuading Lulu to hand *The Apple Star* over because Varaminta was getting somewhere with Dad. And he would only have to let her into the house just once, and *The Apple Star* could be in Varaminta's hands. No matter how pleased Lulu was with her new hiding place, this thought continued to haunt her.

*

That night, once again, the black cab drew up outside and flashed its headlamps. Once again, Lulu checked that all was clear, then crept out to join Cassandra. Lulu had called her earlier to confirm that the Cupid Cakes plan was definitely going ahead, and now here was Cassandra with all the goodies...all but one.

'I'm afraid there's been a bit of a setback,' Cassandra explained, as soon as Lulu was settled on the cab's velvet seat. 'I was expecting a shipment from China this evening, but it didn't arrive. One of the ingredients for the Anti-Dote is missing.'

'Oh.'

'I'm sorry. It's the Chinese Sha-Fu honey; very important, I'm afraid.' Cassandra noticed the crestfallen look on Lulu's face. 'Don't worry, Lulu! We'll get it soon. And when it comes, I can just put it down the coal chute, as I did with your home protection kit.'

'Do you think you'll have it by Saturday?' asked Lulu, anxiously. 'We were going to use the Cupid Cakes on Sunday afternoon. It's...all arranged.'

'Oh, I should have it by then,' Cassandra reassured her. She showed Lulu all the packages she did have, and made sure she understood what was what. 'And this is the myrrh,' she said finally, handing over the last of the packages.

Lulu was intrigued. 'What exactly is myrrh?' she asked.

'Another memory,' said Cassandra, enigmatically. 'Just as your memories helped you to cry onto your Dum'zani seeds, so the Commiphora tree remembers its tragedy and cries tears of myrrh.'

Lulu was always fascinated when Cassandra talked like this; she seemed to view the world in such a different way from everyone else. Like the time she had stated quite plainly that plants talked to each other, just as if it was the most commonplace fact in the world. And Lulu supposed that if this was true – well, then, plants could have memories too, couldn't they, or else they wouldn't have anything to talk about.

'And why does the Commif-whatsit tree cry?' Lulu asked.

'Because it was once a woman, Myrrha, who was transformed into a tree by Venus. Venus did this to protect Myrrha and her unborn child from certain death, and it worked; from the tree sprang the infant Adonis, god of love. But to this day, the tree weeps in memory of the human life it gave for him.'

Much as she enjoyed hearing such stories, Lulu suddenly began to despair. She thought of the characters in the school play, all loving and hating each other in turns; of Jake's sad yearning for Glynnie, and Zena's undignified obsession with Jake. 'Oh, why does love always have to be so full of misery?' she cried. 'I want Dad to be *happy* – oops!' Lulu clapped a hand to her mouth; it embarrassed her that Cassandra should know he was the one she intended to use the Cupid

Cakes on. She wasn't sure she would approve.

Cassandra smiled a secret smile, then hid her amusement. 'Of course you do,' she said. 'But you're right; love can sometimes be agony. That's why it's so important to get the recipe right, Lulu!' She took hold of her hand to emphasise this point. 'As long as you do that, the love will be joyous, rapturous! That is a very special gift to give someone.'

'Uh, thanks,' muttered Lulu, still not knowing where to look.

Cassandra patted her hand. 'You'd better get back inside. Good luck, Lulu. And don't worry too much; if it doesn't go right, you've always got the Anti-Dote. Just make *sure* you wait for that Sha-Fu honey. Good-bye!'

Octopus

Lulu heard nothing from Cassandra all day Thursday. 'Never mind,' said Frenchy. 'You're bound to hear tomorrow.'

On Friday morning, Costas, the gardener, came. Lulu just had time to show him her new plants before leaving for school. 'They're not weeds,' she explained. 'I planted them myself.' Lulu found she had grown so attached to her plants, she had even got into the habit of talking to them. I'm turning into another Cassandra! she thought. She found the idea rather appealing.

Costas scratched his bald head as he stared at the Dum'zani plant. 'Ay ay ay, never I see likey that!' he exclaimed. 'Where you get?'

'Oh, a friend got it for me,' said Lulu, truthfully.

Costas rubbed a leaf between his stubby, hairy fingers. 'Is what, a veggy-tubble?'

'Oh no, it's nothing in particular,' said Lulu; the last

thing she wanted was for him to start asking for vegetables to take home.

*

When Lulu got home after the play rehearsal that afternoon, she immediately checked her phone for messages: nothing. Now she was beginning to worry. She sent Cassandra a text message:

ANY NEWS YET?

...and waited for a reply. And waited. Dad was out – having dinner with the people from the English Apple Marketing Board. At least, Lulu very much hoped he was, and not seeing Varaminta in secret. Lulu drifted restlessly between her bedroom, the kitchen and the living room, where Phil was playing Aileen his band's latest CD.

'I need your lurv,' went the song, 'but you're a cold cold fish'. Lulu wandered into the kitchen, thinking she might have a snack. She opened the fridge door, changed her mind, and closed it again.

'Hey, kiddo,' Aileen called over the din, as she walked into the kitchen. 'You look glum, what's the matter?'

'Oh, nothing,' said Lulu.

'Oi!' called Phil from the living room. 'The best

bit's coming up!'

'All right!' called Aileen, rolling her eyes at Lulu.

Lulu managed a half-smile. 'You'd better go back in there, or he'll get annoyed.'

'Not until you tell me what's up,' said Aileen, resting her hand on Lulu's shoulder.

'Oi, this is the best bit!' called Phil.

'I'm fine,' said Lulu. But Aileen clearly wasn't going to be fobbed off, so she added, 'I just hope Dad's not seeing Varaminta again.'

'Oh, is this because she showed up at that art thing?' Lulu had told Aileen all about that, although she'd missed out the part about Torquil.

'Yes.'

'I'm gonna wrap my tentacles around ya, 'cos I'm your octopus, babe.'

'Phil, turn it down a bit, willya?'

Phil didn't turn it down. Instead, he sang loudly, 'I'm your octopus, BABE...here comes my drum solo!'

Crash wallop crash crash! went the drums, followed by a writhing, electronic octopus-tentacle noise that sounded like *splipple-ipple-ilch*!

Aileen steered Lulu towards the door. 'Come on, girl. If he won't shut up, we'll just go outside.'

They went into the back garden. One small portion of shrubbery remained drenched in the low sun's honey-dipped light, divinely resplendent against the blue-green shadows. 'Don't worry, kid,' Aileen went on. 'I'm sure your dad wouldn't lie. If he says he's seeing the apple people, I'm sure that's what he's doing.'

'Yeah, I guess you're right,' said Lulu, perching on a garden seat.

Splipple-ipple-ilch!

'Oh, Phil!' said Aileen crossly. 'Strewth, he won't give it a rest, will he?'

Squipple-ipp!

Lulu's eyes turned to saucers as she realised the sound wasn't coming from indoors at all. Gazing past Aileen into the sunlit corner, she saw that the Dum'zani plant's growth was now accelerating at an astonishing rate. *Splipple!* it went, as it sent forth a little blue cob, like a flower in a time-lapse nature film.

'Oh!' gasped Lulu, inadvertently. Then she quickly corrected herself. 'No, he won't, er, will he!' She stood up. 'Um, but actually, I rather like it. Let's go back and listen, shall we?'

Splipple-ipp!

Aileen turned to look behind her. 'What was that?'

'Oh it's just the, er...' At that moment, Sushi appeared atop the fence-post, sniffing curiously at the Dum'zani plant. '...Cat!' Lulu breathed a sigh of relief.

She linked arms with Aileen, and guided her swiftly towards the kitchen door.

Behind them, another blue cob *splipped* forth in Sushi's face. *Yeeao-owl!* screeched the cat, and she shot away like a bullet, ears flat against her head.

Aileen shook her head. 'That cat!' she said. 'She's completely bonkers.'

*

'Lulu?'

'Yes!' said Lulu, sitting bolt upright in bed as she answered her phone. She had just fallen asleep, gazing at the Truth Star.

It was Cassandra. 'I'm sorry to bother you so late.'

'No no, that's OK, have you got it?' Lulu asked, her words falling over each other.

Cassandra's voice sounded tinny. 'No, I'm sorry, I haven't. My supplier had an accident; that's why the shipment of Sha-Fu honey from China didn't arrive on Wednesday. They rescheduled it for today, but now it seems they won't be able to make it until next week.'

Lulu shut her eyes. No no no!

'I think you'll have to cancel your tea party,' Cassandra was saying. 'Lulu? Are you there?'

Lulu opened her eyes. 'Yes.'

'I'm really sorry.'

'Oh, that's OK,' said Lulu, flatly.

'It's only a few more days,' said Cassandra. 'You will cancel it, won't you? It's very important.'

'Yes, of course,' said Lulu. 'Thanks. I'll talk to you next week, then. Bye.' She hung up, and almost immediately the phone rang again.

It was Frenchy. 'Lu, how come you didn't call? Are we still on?'

'Um...' Lulu fiddled with her bedsheet.

'Only I've had a look at Mum's diary,' Frenchy added. 'I checked what we thought might be the next available weekend, and she's away on some course; I'm going to be staying with Dad. Then the weekend after that we're going to my gran's...'

'Oh,' said Lulu. She consulted her calendar. With the other weekends already booked up, that meant four...no, *five* weeks, before they might get together. It would be past the best time of the year for it by then, according to the recipe – and after that, it would be the end of term, which was when she and Dad would be going on summer holiday.

But why not go ahead with it anyway – without the Candy-Coated Anti-Dote? She had all the ingredients for the Cupid Cakes, didn't she? And it wasn't as if she had no experience; she'd follow Ambrosia May's instructions to the letter, just as she had with the Truth Cookies. What could possibly go wrong? The Dum'zani corn was at the peak of ripeness and beside herself and Frenchy, it would just be Dad and Jill in the house, nobody else. It wasn't like in the Shakespeare play, with all those Athenians popping up all over the wood and getting in the way. It was *bound* to succeed; she wouldn't need the Anti-Dote then anyway, and Cassandra need never know.

'Lu?'

Lulu turned her back on the Truth Star guiltily. 'Yes,' she said at last. 'We're on.'

Love Hearts

Lulu pulled on a big, baggy T-shirt. Across the chest was the word '**Gutted**', and underneath was an all-too-realistic illustration of a dagger cutting open a belly, with intestines spilling out. She went downstairs for breakfast.

Dad took one look at her and winced. 'Eurgh, that's disgusting!'

Lulu giggled. 'Really gross, isn't it? It's a freebie from Phil – you know, Aileen's boyfriend?'

Dad took a gulp of coffee and grimaced. 'Just because it's free, doesn't mean you have to wear it!'

'Yeah, well, I've got gardening and cooking to do,' said Lulu, taking a carton of milk from the fridge, 'so I thought I'd wear something that doesn't matter.'

'Is that the name of his band then, "Gutted"?'

'Uh-huh. They're really, er...'

'Gross?'

'Er, yup.'

'He's a nice guy though, surely?'

'Well, he doesn't say an awful lot. And he's *really* into his music...'

'I noticed that too,' said Dad. 'He's a bit boring, isn't he? Not quite good enough for our Aileen.' Dad sat down with a plate of toast. 'Oh, cover that thing up, will you? You're putting me off my breakfast.'

Lulu pulled her chair close to the table so he didn't have to look at the T-shirt. Now to get down to business. 'So how was your dinner with the English Apple people?' she asked.

Dad waved his hand dismissively and crunched into his toast. 'Oh, dull.'

Not good enough, thought Lulu. She needed specifics; only then might she be reassured that he hadn't been on a secret date with Varaminta. 'Oh, come on, tell me about it! Where did you go, who was there, what did you talk about?'

Dad raised an eyebrow at her. 'Why are you so interested?'

'I'm just making conversation, Dad! You know, like you do.'

So Dad answered all her questions, Lulu scrutinising him all the while. When he had finished, she wasn't sure she was any the wiser. If I had a Truth Cookie knocking around, she thought, that would soon do the trick. But then, why worry? Another twenty-four hours, and the Cupid Cakes would sort things out, once and for all!

Dad downed the last of his coffee. 'Right, I'm going to take a shower.'

'Make that a bath, Dad,' suggested Lulu.

'Why, am I that smelly?'

Lulu laughed. 'No, just...take your time. Relax. Read the paper. I'll be in here cooking some yummy stuff for tomorrow.'

'Oh, you want me out of the way, is that it?'

'Um...yes.'

Dad kissed her on the head on his way out. 'Noodle, you do take good care of your old dad, don't you?'

More than you know, thought Lulu.

*

The most suitable location for the use of love recipes is in the home. Outdoor locations are only advisable if they are in remote areas, where you can be sure there will be no passers-by. Make sure there are no pictures of others visible, as these too can interfere with the process. Timing is important as well; try to schedule your session for a time when you are least likely to have unexpected visitors. Above all, unless you yourself are taking the love recipe, you must make sure you are out of sight! Even with all these precautions, things can go wrong. For this reason, it is absolutely essential to have an anti-dote ready and to hand.

From the 'Matters of the Heart' section in
The Apple Star, by Ambrosia May

*

'Twenty-two, twenty-three, twenty-four...' Lulu watched as the vivid purple, heartsease-flower essence splashed from the eyedropper onto her cake mixture. As she did so, she thought of the fairy king's words from *A Midsummer Night's Dream*; 'Yet marked I where the bolt of Cupid fell: it fell upon a little western flower, before milk-white, now purple with love's wound'...and felt a shiver of anticipation.

She had already harvested some of her Dum'zani corn with great care, as instructed in *The Apple Star*, touching only the cobs and not the stems. The little blue cobs had crumbled easily between her fingers, into the bowl that already contained the dolphin butter, the perfect little doves' eggs, Lada flour, fragrant almond-blossom honey and chopped dates. Next she had added the powdered boyambe bark, which had a sort of cinnamon/musky forest smell, the grains of paradise for Dad and the dried Osun plantain flakes, which were similar to banana chips, for Jill.

Now Lulu stirred in the myrrh and the rich rose-coloured cocoa-grape wine and watched as they merged with the blue Dum'zani corn and purple heartsease essence, forming swirls of colour in the otherwise beige batter. As she did so, she could swear she saw little, pulsating, heart shapes forming. She blinked and looked again; yes, there they were, pinky-purple blobs like little shiny balloons, trailing their swirly tails. Then they were gone. Absorbed by the mixture that now took on the colour of lilacs.

Fantastic! thought Lulu, having quite forgotten her worries about the Anti-Dote. She felt the way she had as a five-year-old, baking a cake with her mum; completely enthralled with the magic of it all.

Carefully, Lulu spooned the mixture into the cup cake tray, and put it in the oven. Straight away, she took *The Apple Star* back upstairs and returned it to its hiding place. Brilliant, she thought; and Dad hadn't even emerged from his bath yet. She put away the bag that had contained the Cupid Cake ingredients. Now all that remained in it were the ingredients for the Candy-Coated Anti-Dote – all but the Chinese honey. Lulu felt a twinge of guilt, for having disregarded Cassandra's – and Ambrosia May's – advice. Then she took a deep breath; but nothing can go wrong, she told herself. She reminded herself of Cassandra's words; *If the Sun and Moon should doubt, they'd immediately go out*. Surely *believing* all would go well was half the battle, as it had been with the home protection ritual?

Yes, surely.

Apples and Honeysuckle

'Guess they'll be here soon,' said Dad, glancing up from his English Apple documents to check his watch.

'Yup!' said Lulu who, try as she might, could not stop herself from pacing back and forth and wringing her hands.

Dad frowned and scratched his head with his pen. 'Ah!' he said, and jotted down another note to himself. 'Mustn't forget to ask her about that...' he muttered. He was deeply immersed in his thoughts, which was just as well as it meant he didn't notice Lulu's nervous agitation.

Suddenly, the phone rang, making them both jump. 'I'll get it!' said Lulu, and made a dash for the receiver before Dad had a chance to answer it himself.

'Hello?' she said, with all the casual calm she could muster.

'T – minus ten minutes,' came Frenchy's whisper down the phone.

'Oh, it's for me,' Lulu told Dad, before rushing

upstairs and out of earshot. 'Hi,' she said into the receiver, as she closed her bedroom door. 'All systems go.'

'We're just leaving now,' said Frenchy. 'I even got Mum to wear something that's not ten years old and full of moth holes! And guess what; we've had no lentils or lettuce for nearly a week, so fingers crossed, there's no damage done. Now, let's go over this once again. Your dad will make the tea, right?'

'Yes.'

'Then they go and sit in the living room.'

'Uh-huh. And while he was making the tea, I will have put the cakes and plates out on the coffee table.'

'Oh, good, OK. Then we make ourselves scarce, right?'

'Yeah. And we'll be able to spy on things from the garden, through the French windows. There were a couple of pictures I've had to hide; of me, and of Mum...there was even one with Dad in it.'

'Oh boy, imagine if he saw *that*...he'd be mooning around and staring at himself, like Narcissus!'

'Don't even go there. Luckily, he hasn't noticed that I moved them, he's so wrapped up in this English Apple thing.'

Lulu heard Jill's voice in the background. 'Oh, gotta go!' said Frenchy.

'OK, see you in a bit. Bye!'

*

'It's really nice of you to do this,' said Dad to Jill, as he guided her and Frenchy into the house.

'Oh, not at all,' said Jill. 'I'm very into all this stuff; Lulu probably told you. And anyway, these two can't stay away from each other, can they?'

Dad chuckled. 'They are pretty inseparable.'

So will you two be, before long, thought Lulu, beaming angelically at them both.

'Well, come through,' said Dad, 'and I'll get the kettle on.'

They all followed him into the kitchen. 'Ooh, look at those,' said Jill, admiring the tray full of Cupid Cakes. 'Very...unusual!'

'Yes, Lulu's such an inventive cook,' said Dad, reaching for the teapot. 'Always mucking about in the kitchen, aren't you, Noodle?'

'Yup,' said Lulu, picking up the tray. 'I'll take these through.'

Frenchy followed her into the living room. She squeezed Lulu's arm and made an excited little squeaky sound. 'This is it, Lu!' she said, jumping around like an Easter bunny. 'This is The Moment! Oh, I'm so excited I could die. Couldn't you, Lu?'

'Uh-huh,' said Lulu, who was still more tense than anything. She put the tray down on the coffee table and began pacing back and forth again. She still hadn't said anything to Frenchy about the Candy-Coated Anti-Dote.

'Lu, I can't tell you how much I appreciate this,' Frenchy carried on, nineteen-to-the-dozen, following Lulu around the room. 'I mean, you really are the best friend anyone could have in the whole world. Just think! No more Bay-zil Creepy-Face...no more Varaminta for *sure*, no more—'

'Hey, listen,' interrupted Lulu. 'Here they come!'

'...Trying to grow that variety in the allotment at the moment,' Jill was saying to Lulu's dad as they came into the living room. 'It would be tragic if it became extinct.'

'I couldn't agree more,' said Dad, kicking the door to behind him and carrying the tinkling tray of tea things. 'I tasted one the other day, they're delicious!' He set the tray next to the cakes on the coffee table. 'All right girls, ready for some tea?'

'Oh, I'm not really hungry right now, thanks,' said Frenchy.

'Me neither,' said Lulu. 'We'll come back a bit later, OK, Dad? We're going to practise some dance moves for the play.'

'All right, love,' Dad nodded. He poured the tea. 'So anyway,' he carried on, to Jill, 'I've got some drawings

I'd like you to take a look at...'

Lulu and Frenchy retreated to the kitchen, and out into the back garden. They positioned themselves behind the thicket of honeysuckle that grew around the French windows, waited and watched.

Jill was looking at the drawings, engrossed. Lulu's dad stood next to her, gesticulating a lot. Both held mugs of tea, but were completely ignoring the tray of cakes. Lulu and Frenchy looked on, not moving a muscle. After a few moments, Dad sat down, apparently having finished telling Jill everything she needed to know. Now Jill was talking.

A bee emerged from a honeysuckle flower, right in front of Lulu's nose. Lulu held her breath and imagined she was a statue. The only part of her that moved were her eyeballs, which swivelled around towards Frenchy's eyeballs, which could do no more than return an equally alarmed look.

Dad took a sip of tea and talked some more. Jill nodded, and sipped some tea as well.

The bee hovered happily even closer to Lulu's face. It disappeared into another flower, making a bumbling sound that set her teeth on edge. She tried hard to forget it was there, and concentrate on what was going on in the living room.

Dad reached for the tray, put a Cupid Cake on a

plate and handed it to Jill. Hurray! thought Lulu. At last! Now is the moment; this scene, this everyday, ordinary scene will transform into something wonderful and amazing. What would they do? she wondered. Would it be like in old romantic movies, where the man, about to kiss the woman, enfolds her in his arms and bends her over at ninety degrees, her hair trailing down behind her? Would they dance the tango?

Then...the phone rang. It took a moment for it to register with Lulu that the ringing was coming from upstairs. 'Oh, French!' she squeaked. 'I left the phone upstairs after you rang!' She turned to leave. 'I've got to answer it—'

'Shh, no you don't!' hissed Frenchy, grabbing her by the arm and pulling her backwards. 'You'll get in the way! Hang tight, let your dad answer it. He'll be back.'

BZZZZZ! went the bee near Lulu's ear, dislodged from its flower by all the commotion. 'Aah!' squealed Lulu, jumping out of the way. Frenchy shooed it away. Lulu sighed with relief, and the two of them shifted further back from the window, deeper into the honeysuckle bush. What if they'd been heard? The phone stopped ringing. Lulu could barely see into the room now. 'Has Dad gone to answer it?' she whispered to Frenchy.

'I guess...I don't see him.'

Lulu craned her neck forward; she was just able to make out the figure of Frenchy's mum stepping closer and peering curiously in their direction. She couldn't be sure, but she thought it looked as if Jill was eating the cake. Lulu pulled back even further, and for a moment she couldn't even see into the room. She hoped this meant Jill couldn't see her, either. When she felt she could risk it, she peeked inside again and was relieved to see that Jill had retreated a little way.

Relax, she told herself. Dad will come back downstairs, and everything will be as it was. A few moments' delay wouldn't make any difference at all; Jill would still be the first person Dad saw, and Dad would still be the first person Jill saw. No damage done.

Then a different ringing sound started; muted, distant. No, it can't be, thought Lulu. Suddenly, she was hot and cold at the same time: oh, yes, it could. The doorbell.

'French, I *have* to go and answer that!'

Frenchy looked green. 'GO!' was all she could say.

Lulu dashed back into the kitchen and out into the hallway, with Frenchy close behind her. Just in time to see Jill opening the front door.

Crumbs

Four people stood in the hallway, not moving a hair. The two girls, stunned, stared at the two adults. The woman stared at the man, and the man stared at the woman. The man held a large, flat object encased in bubble wrap. He put it down and rested it against the wall.

'What are you doing here?' he said to the woman at last.

'I...' stammered Jill.

'Here, Jill, you all right?' asked the man. 'You look peculiar!'

Frenchy took hold of Lulu's hand and squeezed it. 'Dad!' she whispered.

Lulu was groaning inwardly. No, no, this is all wrong! But at the same time, she knew that Frenchy was probably saying to herself, Yes, yes, this is even more perfect!

'You...you'd better come in,' said Jill, stepping aside. She sounded as if she were in a trance.

'I was just passing,' said Jack. 'Mike bought this painting, see, and so happens I was delivering another one nearby. Is he in?'

'Y-yes...*Jack*,' said Jill, breathily. 'Uh, Mike's on the phone.'

Jack cocked his head to one side and peered at Jill. 'Is something up? Is Amanda here – oh hallo, love,' he added, as he noticed his daughter over by the kitchen door.

'Hi, Dad,' said Frenchy, stepping forward.

'Hi, Lulu,' said Jack.

'Hi,' Lulu managed, although she felt as if she'd turned to stone.

Jill was still transfixed by Jack, gazing at him as if she were noticing for the first time ever the crinkly blue-eyed smile, the broad shoulders, the strong hands.

Jack glanced from Jill to Frenchy. 'What you done to your mum, then, eh?' he joked.

'Nothing!' said Frenchy, a little too forcefully. 'I mean, uh...' She trailed off, dumbfounded.

Lulu glanced upstairs, aware that Dad seemed to be taking rather a long time up there. Hadn't he heard the doorbell?

'Well, let's get this painting in, shall we?' said Jack, picking up the package. 'Your dad wanted it on the wall above a couch, I believe...' he went on, Jill trailing behind him like a lovelorn puppy. Lulu hid her anxiety as best she could, while she showed him into the sitting room. 'Oh, nice room,' remarked Jack, putting the package down. He knelt beside it and began pulling off the bubble wrap. 'Be good to see this in situ.'

Lulu caught Frenchy's eye, and jerked her head in the direction of the kitchen.

'Uh...be right back,' said Frenchy, and the two of them disappeared into the kitchen and closed the door.

'I'm sorry, Lu, I had no idea this would happen...'

'I'm beyond that already,' said Lulu, resuming her pacing. 'French, I've just thought...suppose Dad's had some cake already?'

Frenchy frowned. 'Huh?'

'My dad could have had some cake, don't you see? We were distracted by that bee, right around the time he left the room, so we don't know whether he did or not. Even if he only took one bite, that might be enough to affect him...'

'Oh boy, I see what you mean,' said Frenchy. 'Better give him the Anti-Dote quick, then,' she added, her eyes searching the room.

Lulu's face flushed.'Um...' She braced herself for her confession.

'You *have* got the Anti-Dote?'

'Well, that's the thing, I...that is, you see, er...no.'

Frenchy gasped. 'But you said...'

'I know, and I *was* telling the truth. It's just that there was this missing ingredient, and then you said about your mum being away, and...well, I just...' Lulu paused as, panic-stricken, she heard Dad's voice coming from the next room. 'Oh good grief, he's back down!' she cried.

'Oh blimey,' said Frenchy. 'Hey, Lu, don't worry,' she added brightly, grabbing Lulu's arm. 'Don't forget, he probably *didn't* eat any cake. I really don't think he had time.'

A little glimmer of hope brightened a corner of Lulu's mind. 'French, I so hope you're right.' The two girls headed back into the living room. But the scene that greeted them filled Lulu with horror.

The couch was pulled away from the wall, and Jack's large, abstract painting, now uncovered, leaned against the wall. Jill stood on the far side of the couch, still gazing at Jack. Lulu's dad stood beside the coffee table, a half-eaten cake in his hand. Kneeling beside the couch was Jack, his head and shoulders obscured by the picture he was holding. It was a picture of Varaminta – and Dad was looking right at it.

'*Aaargh!*'

Everyone turned and stared at Lulu.

Lulu did her best to compose herself. 'S-sorry. It's just that...where the heck did that thing come from?!'

'It was behind the couch,' explained Jack, his face appearing from behind the Varaminta picture. 'We were moving the couch so's we could hold the picture up there, see how it looks.'

'It...must have been accidentally left behind by the movers...' said Dad. Lulu noticed grimly that he spoke in exactly the same trance-like way as Jill had done, moments before. This is unbearable, she thought. Never again, she told herself; never again will I do this.

Frenchy took hold of her hand. 'Chill out, Lu,' she whispered.

Yes, chill out, Lulu told herself. It's not the end of the world; there's still the Anti-Dote. Just a few more days, and Dad will have the Anti-Dote, and everything will be all right again.

But a lot could happen in a few days...

Jack parked the Varaminta picture in the corner and stood up. He joined Jill beside his painting. 'Shall we?' he said to Jill, gesturing towards it.

Jill gazed at him dreamily. 'Oh, yes, *let's*!' She stood there.

Jack cleared his throat. 'Ahem. The painting...?'

'Oh! Right.' Jill finally leaned down and helped Jack to hoist the canvas aloft.

'How's it look?' Jack called over his shoulder.

Lulu's dad looked like an actor who'd forgotten his

lines. He scratched his head. He pointed vaguely at the Varaminta picture, then rubbed his chin. He shifted this way and that, he gazed at some distant spot, frowning. 'What? Oh, yes. Good...' he muttered eventually.

'Yeah, reckon it'll look the business,' agreed Jack, before prompting Jill to lower the painting to the floor again. He came around to the front of the couch, rubbing his hands together as he eyed the Cupid Cakes. 'Well, Mike,' he said, 'think I'll take you up on the offer of some cake.'

Lulu lunged forward desperately. 'Oh, they're not very nice actually; bit of a failure,' she said, as she whisked them away. 'We've, uh, got some *really* nice biscuits, would you like some?'

Both dads gave her sideways, mildly worried looks.

'Actually,' said Jill loudly, breaking the awkward silence, 'I must be going.' She put her hand to her head. 'I'm sorry, Michael, can we talk another time? I'm...not feeling great.'

'No, that's OK,' replied Lulu's dad, slowly. 'It's not the best time for me, either, as it happens.'

'Jack,' said Jill, her voice wobbling as her eyes became glassy with tears. 'Oh Jack...take me *home*!'

Jack reached over and rested a hand on her shoulder. 'Yes, love. Of course.'

Minty

Lulu watched Dad closely all evening. He was behaving very strangely, but she found it quite impossible to work out what was going on in his head. That night, after much agonising and Truth Star-gazing, she switched on the light, got a pen and paper, and wrote a list:

What Dad's Like
vague
distracted
secretive
sighs a lot
forgetful

She studied the list; it was love, all right. She flopped back onto her pillow. And it had to be Varaminta; he'd been staring directly at her picture. If Varaminta hadn't already made him fall secretly in love with her again,

Lulu had certainly made sure he was now.

'But I must stop thinking about it,' she told the Mum-in-Muddy-Wellies picture. 'He'll be back to normal when I give him the Candy-Coated Anti-Dote anyway; just a few more days to go.' She kept telling herself this, but still she found it impossible to stop thinking of all the terrible things that could happen before then. She sat up again, and made another list:

The Worst That Can Happen
Dad and Varaminta get back together
They fly to Vegas and secretly get married
Varaminta uses Dad to get hold of The Apple
    Star
My secret will be out
Varaminta will try to use The Apple Star for
    her evil ends and who knows what
    disasters will follow

Then, although Dad would fall out of love again once he'd had the Anti-Dote, the damage would be enormous. Even if they didn't actually get married, one thing was for sure; Varaminta would lose no time in using Dad's infatuation to get hold of *The Apple Star*.

*

Frenchy bowled up to Lulu in the classroom on Monday morning. 'Oh, Lu, thankyouthankyouthankyou! A million gazillion thankyous!'

Lulu busied herself with organising her desk. 'All right, don't overdo it,' she said, pretending to be engrossed in the task of organising her history folder. She wanted to be happy for Frenchy – no, she *was* happy for Frenchy – but somehow there wasn't space for Being Happy For Frenchy in her brain right now, because her brain was crammed to overflowing with WORRY.

'Lu, Mum is just crazy about Dad!' Frenchy went on.

'And he's pleased about this, I take it?' said Lulu, glancing up from the pages of her folder.

'Pleased? Lu, he's over the moon. She's the one who booted him out, remember? Because he was in such a bad mood the whole time?'

'Because he was a failure.'

'He was not a failure!' said Frenchy, indignantly. 'Well, all right, maybe he was a bit – back then. Not now. Lu, he stayed for dinner! It's the first time all three of us have eaten together in years! I never realised, but it seems as if Dad's been holding a secret flame for Mum all this time. Now I really think they'll get back together, and it's all thanks to you!'

'Well, that's all right then, isn't it?' Lulu hadn't

meant the tone of sarcasm to creep into her voice, but she couldn't help it. The guilt she felt for this ungenerous remark just added to the leaden gloom she was feeling already, and she felt her face crumple as the tears began to well up. She knew Frenchy didn't mean to rub her nose in it, but that wasn't how it felt.

'Lu, I'm sorry,' said Frenchy, resting a hand on her shoulder.

'No, it's fine!' sniffed Lulu, flicking a page so industriously that a corner tore off.

'Look,' Frenchy whispered, pulling up her chair. 'When will you be able to give your dad the you-know-what?'

Lulu bit her lip. 'Not sure – should be this week.'

'Well there you go! That's not long, is it?'

Lulu put the folder down and turned to face her. 'You don't understand,' she whispered urgently. 'He's going around like some sort of zombie, like he's...hypnotised or something. For all we know, Varaminta can just click her fingers and he'll do whatever she says, including digging out the you-know-what book, and giving it to her.'

'Oh, come on, that won't happen!'

'It *might*.'

Frenchy shrugged. 'OK; lend it to me then. Until you can give him the whatchama-call-it.'

Lulu smiled. 'Oh, French, you're completely brilliant!'

'I know.'

'All I have to worry about now is them running off together for a shotgun wedding.'

*

'How now, spirit, whither wander you?' said Aileen, kneeling on the floor beside Lulu as she put the finishing touches to her fairy costume.

Lulu duly recited: 'Over hill, over dale, through bush, through briar – *ouch*!'

'Oops, sorry, kiddo,' said Aileen, adjusting the pin she had just accidentally spiked Lulu with.

''Sall right,' said Lulu, glumly.

Aileen glanced up. She smiled brightly, and let out a little laugh. 'Haha, you should keep that in; "through bush, through briar – *ouch*!" I mean, it would be a bit prickly, wouldn't it?'

'Hmmm,' said Lulu. She raised her arm to check her watch: 8.15. '*What* time did you say Dad was coming home?'

'Hang on a tick, Lu, put your arm back down a minute...there!' Aileen secured the last of the pins on the dress. 'Your dad'll be home soon enough,' she added. 'He just had to meet someone for a quick drink after work. And you know how late he sometimes works... Now, let's take a look at ya.' She stood up and stepped back to admire her handiwork. 'I think you're gonna make a really ace fairy.'

The doorbell rang. 'That'll be Dad!' cried Lulu, suddenly animated. 'He must've forgotten his key.' She rushed to open the door, and her heart sank; it was Phil. He winked at her – 'All right?'– and strode in, zips a-jangle.

'Oh, hello,' said Lulu, unable to conceal her disappointment. Dad was supposed to have been back at eight; quite late enough as it was, without this further delay. And just who was this 'someone' he was meeting?

Walking back into the living room, Lulu thought she detected a flicker of annoyance on Aileen's face too – whether at Dad for not coming home when he said he would, or at Phil for interrupting her dressmaking session, Lulu couldn't tell. 'Hey,' said Aileen.

'All right?' said Phil, planting a peck on Aileen's forehead. 'Gig on down the Nag's Head; wanna go?'

'Oh, Phil, I'm tired,' said Aileen. 'Do you mind if I don't? And I've got sequins to sew; all right, Lu, you can take that off now – be careful you don't make the pins fall out.'

'OK,' said Lulu, and turned to leave. In her room, she gingerly removed the wispy green frock, and put her pyjamas on. She thought about phoning Cassandra and confessing, then decided against it; phoning wouldn't bring her that missing ingredient any sooner. And she'd rather Cassandra didn't know about what she had done.

She picked up the book at her bedside, *The Twelve Labours of Heracles*. It had become a favourite read, ever since she had discovered the link between Heracles and *The Apple Star*. Cassandra had spoken inspiringly about Heracles's eleventh labour, to retrieve the golden apples of the Hesperides, which were said in the book's introduction to symbolise all that Ambrosia May's magical recipes had to offer. What interested Lulu most about Heracles was not his god-like strength – although that did have a certain fascination – but his cunning. Yes, he could slay the hundred-headed dragon, but he could also out-smart Atlas. She opened the book at a random page: a picture showed Heracles wrestling with the Nemean Lion. She knew the story off by heart: Heracles tried arrows and a sword, but both were powerless against the lion's pelt, which was as tough as armour. So Heracles had resorted to cunning; after clubbing the lion about the head, making it dizzy, he was able to trap it with a net and finally strangle it to death.

Once again, Lulu was reminded of Cassandra's words about the 'meaning behind the myth' – the truth in every story. And the meaning here, as before, was unmistakable: be cunning. Outwit your opponent. Great, thought Lulu, as she stared at the Mum-in-Muddy-Wellies picture; I seem to have failed dismally at that so far, don't I? At least moving *The Apple Star* to Frenchy's would help – otherwise it was just a case of waiting to give Dad the Anti-Dote, for now. But Lulu had the distinct feeling that there would be a need for more cunning before long...

At that moment, she heard Dad come home. She flung the book to the floor, and ran downstairs. 'Dad!' she cried, flinging her arms around him.

'Hi, Noodle,' he said, kissing her on the head and patting her shoulder. But this wasn't the usual greeting Lulu got from him; his mind was obviously somewhere else – and he didn't even apologise for being late. Lulu stood back and watched, crestfallen, as he wandered into the living room, murmured a brief greeting to Aileen and Phil, then drifted upstairs.

She shuffled into the living room, where Aileen was getting ready to leave.

'Got that dress then, kid?' said Aileen.

'Oh. Yeah,' said Lulu. She returned to her

room, retrieved the fairy dress and brought it back downstairs.

Aileen folded it and put it into a plastic bag. 'I'll have this ready for the dress rehearsal, OK, Lu?'

'Uh-huh. Thanks.'

'Hey, about your dad,' Aileen added, on her way out of the door. 'Seems a bit down in the dumps or something. Go and cheer him up, there's a girl.'

'Pub,' prompted Phil to Aileen, taking her hand and jerking his head pub-ward.

'No, Phil, I told you, I've got sewing to do! Seeya, kid.' She rolled her eyes at Lulu and kissed her goodbye.

Lulu closed the door behind them. A beeping sound came from the living room; it sounded like a text message. She went in. There, on the coffee table were: Dad's wallet, Dad's newspaper...and Dad's mobile phone. Its screen was lit up:

1 NEW MESSAGE

Lulu glanced over her shoulder; Dad was apparently still upstairs. She picked up the phone, took a deep breath and hit the button that said 'show'. The words that revealed themselves on the screen filled her with dread:

MIKEY, LOOKING FORWARD 2 SEEING U AT MINE 2MORROW! MINTY XXX

Camomile Tea

There was a gentle knock at the door. 'Time to get up, Lulu.'

'I'm not going to school today,' said Lulu, pulling the duvet over her head. It was the most cunning move she could think of.

She heard Dad come into the room. 'What's the matter?' he asked.

'I've gop a pummy ache,' said Lulu, muffled by the bedding.

'Oh,' said Dad. Even from the darkness of the duvet, Lulu could tell this was not his usual overflowing-with-sympathy response. 'Well, I'll phone Aileen.'

'No!' said Lulu, throwing off the covers and sitting bolt upright. 'Can't you take a day off work?'

'No, I really can't.'

'Oh, but Aileen's got tons of studying to do for her business studies course...*and* she's making my dress—'

'She can do all that here,' said Dad.

Lulu grabbed hold of his arm and hugged it. 'But Dad, *please*! You've been staying late at work, you could take just one day!' She gazed longingly into his eyes. She was aware that she even – shame on her! – fluttered her eyelids with pathos. He *had* to stay home; only then might she be able to prevent him from seeing Varaminta.

Dad heartlessly extracted his arm from her grip. 'NO!' he insisted. 'I'm needed at the office, I'm far too busy. I'm going to call Aileen...' He strode towards the door.

'Take me with you then!' said Lulu quickly, lurching after him as she tripped over the discarded bedding.

Dad turned and gave her a sideways look. 'But you're sick, remember?'

'I could just sit in the corner of your office with a hot water bottle,' said Lulu, kneeling beside him and reaching for his hand. 'I'd be no trouble...*please*, Dad!'

'I said *no*, now stop pestering me!' said Dad crossly, stepping away from her. 'If you're too sick to go to school, you're too sick to come to the office. Do you really have a tummy ache?'

Lulu sat back on her heels. 'Yes,' she said quietly. Put your arms around me, at least! she thought. He was so different, she couldn't bear it. And it was all her fault.

'I'll make you some camomile tea with honey,' said Dad, like a brisk nurse; caring but remote. He left the room.

Lulu picked up her duvet, climbed back onto the bed and curled into a ball. Of course, she didn't have a stomach ache. But her heart ached terribly.

A little while later, Dad returned, dressed for work and carrying the promised cup of camomile tea. He still had the distant look in his eyes that he'd had ever since Sunday afternoon. 'I'm off,' he said. 'Aileen's on her way. Bye.' A cursory peck on the forehead, and he was gone.

At the sound of the front door shutting behind him, Lulu burst into tears. So much for that cunning move; it hadn't worked. Now she just *had* to phone Cassandra; she couldn't bear this any longer.

'Oh, it's all gone horribly wrong!' Lulu wailed down the phone when Cassandra picked up.

'What has? The recipe?'

'It's Dad...he's changed, and I want him back! And he's in love with *her* all over again...oh, it's all such a terrible mess!'

'Wait a minute,' said Cassandra. 'Are you saying you went ahead with the Cupid Cakes without waiting until you had the Anti-Dote?'

Lulu sniffed. 'Yes. I'm sorry, it's just—'

'Lulu, you *promised*—'

'I know, I'm really sorry. But it was the only time we could get them together, and...oh, he's so different, I don't know what to do! Say I can make him right again, I'll do anything, *anything*! I want my Dad ba-ha-hack!' She began to sob uncontrollably.

'All right, sshhh!' said Cassandra. 'Please, listen to me.'

Lulu grabbed a tissue and blew her nose loudly, struggling to hold onto the phone at the same time. 'I'b listedding.'

'I was going to call you anyway; the delivery is due on Thursday. I can't arrange for it to come any sooner, I've already tried that on your behalf. But that's only two days from now. I'll deliver to you straight away, down the coal chute. Then you can make the Anti-Dote, and everything will be all right.'

'Oh, thank you!' Lulu felt better for having told Cassandra; she had so needed some reassurance from her.

'You feel as if your father doesn't love you any more, don't you?' Cassandra added.

'That's right!' said Lulu, dabbing her cheeks with the tissue. 'That's exactly how it feels! He's got no time for me at all; he's distracted and vague...and I feel so *bad*...'

'Well, so you should,' said Cassandra.

'I know,' said Lulu, her chin beginning to wobble again. 'He's right not to love me, I'm horrid.'

'Not horrid, just stupid,' said Cassandra, bluntly.

Stupid, yes.

'...But Lulu, your father loves you just as much as he ever did,' Cassandra added.

'He does?' said Lulu, toying with her grubby tissue.

'Of course he does...but it sounds to me as if he's suffering from unrequited love.'

'Oh, no, that's not true,' said Lulu. 'She *really* wants him back.'

'Hmmm,' mused Cassandra. 'That doesn't fit at all.'

'Why not?'

'Lulu, think about it. Someone newly in love, who is loved in return...they are bursting with joy! That spills over into everything. If your father were happy right now, you'd certainly know it. Take my word for it, he's pining for someone he cannot have.'

'Lulu?' called Aileen from downstairs.

'Hi,' Lulu called back. 'I'd better go,' she whispered to Cassandra. 'I'm really confused now...but thanks all the same.'

'All right, Lulu,' said Cassandra. 'Don't worry...he'll soon be back to normal.'

But as the morning wore on, Lulu became increasingly agitated. She found it hard not to think about the appointment that she knew Dad had arranged with Varaminta. At the same time, Cassandra's words puzzled her. She didn't know how to square the two things.

'Perhaps you should watch a movie or something,' suggested Aileen, interpreting Lulu's restlessness as boredom.

Good idea, thought Lulu; there was a new DVD she hadn't watched yet, and it was a comedy. That ought to cheer her up. Lulu took the new disc and knelt beside the DVD player. But when she opened the disc drive, another unpleasant surprise hit her: there was a disc in the drive, and on it was written:

Varaminta: Sweet Nothings

It was a recording of the advertisement Varaminta and Dad had made together not long after they had met, nearly a year and a half ago. There could be only one reason why this was here, Lulu told herself: Dad had been staying up late at night, gazing at his beloved in private. Then it hit her: this explained why he was so distant. Not because his love was unrequited, but because it was *secret*. He couldn't bring himself to tell Lulu about it – yet – so that meant he couldn't spend all his time with Varaminta, as he'd like to. Hence watching her on the DVD.

Lulu got up and left the room; there was no way she

felt like watching a film now. Instead, her mind turned to ways in which she might be able to come between Dad and Varaminta, just to prevent him doing anything rash before he took the Anti-Dote. I'll call him at work, she decided, as she climbed the stairs. I'll say I'm feeling much worse...it might be acute appendicitis!...and he must come home right away.

Lulu ran to her father's study, picked up the phone and hit the button marked 'office'. The secretary answered. 'Michael Baker's office?'

'Is he there, please?' asked Lulu, putting on her best acute-appendicitis-suffering voice. 'It's Lulu, his daughter. It's urgent.'

'I'm sorry, Lulu,' said the secretary. 'Michael phoned in this morning. He's out of the office all day today.'

Lunch

The next day was Wednesday, which of course meant piano lesson. Lulu and Frenchy walked down the hill together towards the bus stop.

'Sorry I can't go with you to your piano teacher's today,' said Frenchy.

'What? Oh, that,' said Lulu, flatly. 'I don't think Torquil's going to bother me this time. Why should he? Now Dad's fallen for Varaminta, they must think they've got it made.'

'Yes, Lu, but don't forget he'll soon be *out* of love with her again. And your wonderful book is safe with me in the meantime, just in case!' She slapped Lulu on the shoulder, in an effort to cheer her up. *The Apple Star* was now hidden away in Frenchy's room, locked in her 'safe'; really just a money box in the shape of a house. The book *just* fitted inside.

They arrived at the bus stop. 'Well, see you tomorrow,' said Frenchy. 'I've got to get straight home.

Mum needs all the moral support she can get right now, so I don't want to be home late.'

'Why? What's up?'

'Oh, it's that Basil; she's dumped him, of course, but he's freaked her out. You'll never guess what he did yesterday. He was there, waiting on the doorstep with a bunch of flowers, when we got home. Mum was really nice and everything; you know, can't let you come in, I'm really sorry, da-dada, but he just barged his way in and followed us up the stairs. Ugh, you should have heard him! "Eaoh, Jill, we're perfect for each other, you kneaow that!" The neighbours saw it all.'

'How embarrassing.'

'There's more,' said Frenchy. 'When we got to our front door, Dad was waiting outside with a much bigger bunch of flowers, and a box of chocs. And before Mum knew what was happening, he'd swooped her up in his arms. It was dead romantic!'

'What did Basil do then?'

'He went crazy. Lu, we were absolutely right about him. He starting ranting and raving, calling Mum a scarlet woman—'

'What?!'

'Yeah, it was awful. Dad had to turf him out. So she just doesn't want to be on her own at the moment.' There was the sound of approaching voices, and

Frenchy turned. 'Oh, don't look now but it's the Zena Lemon gang...looks like they're giving Glynnie a hard time again.'

'Give them back!' demanded Glynnie, as she turned and stopped in front of the others.

'I ain't got 'em,' said Zena, insolently flicking a piece of gum around her large mouth. Lulu could see that there was some surreptitious passing around going on among the tight-knit group. Since Glynnie wasn't wearing her glasses, it was a fair bet that Zena had snatched them off her.

'Don't look at me,' said Chantrelle, shrugging.

'She ain't lookin' atcha,' quipped Zena. 'She's just lookin' at the end of her nose; vat's as far as she can see, innit!' The whole gang found this remark utterly hilarious.

At that moment the bus arrived, and Zena and co. were suddenly distracted by their ritual scuffle to be the first to get on. Glynnie's spectacles clattered to the ground. Lulu shot her hand in among the thundering feet, and retrieved them. 'Here you are, Glyn,' she said, handing them back.

'Thanks, Lu,' said Glynnie. Hands shaking, she dusted the glasses on her sweatshirt, and put them on. One arm of the glasses was bent, making them sit wonkily on her face.

Frenchy took Glynnie's arm. 'Come on, Glyn. You're sitting with me. I'll see you tomorrow, Lu.'

'Yeah,' said Lulu, gazing after them. ''Bye.' Horrible girls! she thought, as she headed off down the road. She felt guilty; perhaps she could have done more to help Glynnie. She seemed to remember there being a recipe in *The Apple Star* that improved eyesight. But she'd been so wrapped up in her own situation, she'd failed to notice that she could be helping someone else. And then she'd gone and mucked up her own little scheme anyway. Not very clever.

But how much would it help to improve Glynnie's eyesight for a few days, anyway? Even if it were possible to improve it permanently – and she had no idea whether it was – it wouldn't stop them teasing her. They'd only find something else to taunt Glynnie about, because their poisonous jealousy made them hate her. Was there a recipe for getting rid of hatred, Lulu wondered. It was all very well trying to get this one to fall in love with that one, but how did you stop people from hating?

Lulu was so wrapped up in her thoughts, she'd completely forgotten about Torquil. So seeing him leaning against a cherry tree in front of her was something she was quite unprepared for.

'Thought I'd find you here,' he said, with his usual

smirk. 'Not got your mate with you today?'

'No,' said Lulu. 'Look, why can't you just leave me alone?'

'Oh, I will, I will, don't you worry,' said Torquil. He seemed inordinately pleased with himself. 'Just came to let you know it's all over. Mission accomplished! This time tomorrow, we'll be on the road to Millionaires-ville – and you won't see a scrap of it. You've missed your chance. Too bad, eh?'

Lulu felt as if she were going to be sick. But, he's bluffing, he's bluffing! she kept telling herself. Even if Dad had let Varaminta into their house today, *The Apple Star* wasn't there. No; not until Lulu knew for certain that Varaminta and Torquil had her magical book, would she ever own up about it. She did her best to steady her voice as she replied, 'Torquil, you've been watching too many thrillers. I think you live in a complete fantasy world. Goodbye.' She marched on ahead, but Torquil kept pace with her.

'You had your little triumph, that day at St Toast's, didn't you?' he went on. 'There was something in those cookies you gave me, turned me into a wacko supergrass – and as for my mum, well, she suffered *big* time. The gossip columns had a field day. "She's got a screw loose", they said.' Torquil twisted a finger at his temple. '"She's cracked; out to lunch." But that's the thing, isn't it? Sometimes people might *seem* out to lunch, when they're not at all. Isn't that right, Poodle? Well, seeya round.' And he was gone.

At least the tormenting was over for another day. Lulu shuddered. 'It's all lies,' she said aloud. Lies, lies, lies. 'Mission accomplished': what rot, she thought, as she went through her piano instructor's garden gate. How could the 'mission' possibly be 'accomplished', with the book safely hidden – even if Dad was under Varaminta's spell? Tuh!

She walked up the garden path.

And as for Varaminta, well, she really *did* have a screw loose.

Lulu reached the front door.

Varaminta didn't just *seem* out to lunch, she really *was*...

Lulu stopped.

Out to lunch.

'Oh...no...'

Leg of Lamb Yard

Lulu rushed back down her piano teacher's garden path and headed towards the bus stop. As she ran, she remembered another door, one with a notice on it: *Out to Lunch. Back in 5 mins.*

At least that was what it had seemed to say. But of course it hadn't, had it? A handwritten scrawl, the words had in fact been:

> **Otto Lunch**
>
> **Bockin Smins**

...the names of the proprietors of the strangest bookshop ever. *The* bookshop; the one Varaminta had found Lulu in on that extraordinary birthday when she had run away. The one where *The Apple Star* had literally fallen into her hands...

Sometimes people might seem *out to lunch, when they're not at all. Isn't that right, Poodle?*

Torquil was giving her a clue! Not out of any desire

to help her, of course, oh no...he was enjoying tormenting her. Mission accomplished...that didn't mean, 'Varaminta's got *The Apple Star*'. No. It meant, 'Varaminta's worked out where you got the book in the first place, and has gone back to get another one like it.'

Lulu was gasping for breath as she reached the end of the street, and her mind was racing. How would she find her way to Mister O's shop? She had found it by accident before. Well, she hadn't worked that part out yet; all she knew right now was that she had to do something, and she certainly wasn't going to her piano lesson.

Lulu thought about what Mister O had said that day, about books finding people in his shop, instead of the other way round. If Varaminta was going there to *find* a book, what chance did she really have of succeeding? And even if Mister O did sometimes find books for people, would he remember Varaminta from before, and refuse to help? He was on Lulu's side, surely. Then again, it had been a whole year ago. The more Lulu thought about it, the more unsettled she felt about everything. Torquil had been so confident; and who knew what was possible at Mister O's strange shop? And what if they harmed him too?

There were phone calls to make. Lulu had her mobile phone in her backpack. She called her piano teacher, saying that she suddenly felt very ill. Well, it's the truth, she told herself; just not the whole truth. When she had finished with that call, she rang Aileen, and told her she was getting a lift home from the piano teacher. There; she was a free agent for the next hour. After that...well, she would worry about that when the time came. Right now she was more concerned with how on earth she would find the shop. Was Mister O reachable by telephone? Any normal business would be, of course, but Mister O's had felt like a time-warp. And sure enough, when she tried directory enquiries, there was no listing.

Lulu sighed and slipped the phone back into her backpack just as she reached the bus stop. She had to cross the road, to take the bus heading into town; that much she did know. A bus arrived, destined for 'Aldwych'; she got on, flashed her bus pass, and took a seat.

Aldwych. Old Witch, thought Lulu, nervously. Would it take her anywhere near where she wanted to go? The bus was crowded with weary shoppers, noisy schoolkids, and some even noisier backpackers, chattering excitedly in a foreign language. A tiny old lady in black sat nearby, her face brown and crinkled like a walnut. She met Lulu's gaze, unnervingly, with surprisingly stark blue eyes. Lulu looked away and stared out of the window; café, shop, pub. Think. What else was on the same street as Mister O's shop? *Pub*. Yes, there had been a pub, one with a distinctive sign. Something green...a frog! That was it; Lulu was sure the pub had been called simply 'The Frog'; if she tried directory enquiries again, maybe she could get the street name. She took out her phone.

'Directory, which name, please?'

'The Frog; um, it's a pub,' said Lulu, feeling a bit daft.

'Which town please?'

'London.'

'I have a listing in WC1...would that be it?'

'What street is it on?'

'Leg of Lamb Yard—'

'Great, thank you!' Lulu hung up before the operator could even give her the number. Fantastic! Now all she had to do was find Leg of Lamb Yard. She glanced up, and noticed immediately an *A-Z* book that one of the backpackers was now consulting.

Lulu leaned forward. 'Excuse me?' she said, pointing at the *A-Z*. 'Could I just quickly look something up?'

The bearded youth regarded her blankly. *'Scusi?'*

At this point the walnut-faced lady intervened, waving a gnarled finger in their direction. *'Il libro, il libro!'* she said in a crackly, high-pitched voice. *'Vuole farsi prestare il libro.'*

'Ah!' said the backpacker at last, and handed

Lulu the *A-Z*.

Lulu thanked them both profusely, and looked up Leg of Lamb Yard. Not surprisingly, there was just one. And, amazingly, it was near Holborn tube station, not very far from the Aldwych. She pulled a scrap of paper from her backpack and attempted a very crude map, copying from the *A-Z*, then handed it back to the young man and thanked him again. She smiled at the old lady, who smiled back, nodding slowly. Her astonishing eyes twinkled. *Old witch*...now that Lulu thought of it, perhaps this was a good omen after all. There was such a thing as a good witch, after all, wasn't there?

Lulu consulted her watch: 4.20. If she wasn't home by 5.15 at the latest, Aileen would start to worry. She got up and wove her way along the lurching bus towards the driver. 'Um, excuse me, but does this bus stop at Holborn tube station?'

'Yep,' said the driver.

'Um, well, do you know what time we'll get there?'

The driver sniffed, glancing wearily at his clock. ''Bout twenty to,' he said, tersely.

'Oh, good...um, could you let me know when we're there? Please?'

The driver sniffed again. 'Yeah.'

'Thanks!'

*

Lulu knew instantly that she had the right place. Seeing the cobbled street again, the pub reassuringly where it was supposed to be, gave her a fizz of excitement, in spite of the dread she still felt. An old man sat outside The Frog; he had just a few strands of hair plastered to his shiny head, and a sweaty, warty face. He regarded Lulu with detachment as she passed by, took a sip of beer and burped.

Lulu rushed past and round the corner and there, two doors down, was the familiar stuffed owl greeting her from the window of Mister O's shop. She ran to the door and knocked. Then she noticed the doorbell and rang that too. She waited. She had expected to have to wait, but this was taking longer than it was supposed to. Or did it just seem that way, because she was in such a fluster? She rang and knocked again. 'Hello? Mister O?'

Nothing.

'He's shut,' said a voice.

Lulu turned around; it was the man outside the pub who spoke.

'Shut up shop, what, twenty minutes ago,' said the man. 'Gone home.'

'Oh no!' cried Lulu.

'Mmm, bit early,' said the man who, Lulu now

noticed, bore an uncanny resemblance to the frog on the pub sign. 'But I've noticed he keeps odd hours, that chap.'

Lulu stared in disbelief at the shop window and the stuffed owl in it, which seemed to be gloating over her misfortune.

'You could always come back tomorrow,' said Mr Frog. Widening his bulgy eyes, he looked even more froggish.

'No, you don't understand,' said Lulu. 'I was...there was someone...oh, good grief!' She shook her head in despair. She thought for a moment, then said, 'Has anyone been to the shop, while you've been sitting here?'

'Matter of fact, two ladies came by not so long ago – one of 'em was a real corker too.'

'Oh, no! Tall, blonde?'

'That's the one!' said Mr Frog, taking another slug of beer.

'And the other woman?'

Mr Frog shuddered. 'Ugh, no! Shaped like a tank, that one, face like a bulldog.'

Grodmila! thought Lulu. So she was right; Grodmila *was* part of Varaminta's team, and brought along, no doubt, to help identify the book for her.

'Lucky devil,' chuckled Mr Frog.

'What?' said Lulu.

'That chap – Otto, is it?'

'Little and old, with glasses?' said Lulu, to make sure they were talking about the same person, and not the mysterious Mr Smins, Mister O's partner.

'Yes, that's him; never seen the other one, actually,' said Mr Frog. 'Well, old Otto followed them out of the shop, to lock up. Tickled pink, the blonde one was; he must've found the lady *just* what she was looking for. "Oh, *dahling*, how can I ever thank you!" she was saying, over and over.' Lulu was struck by how very like Varaminta he sounded. '*Hugging* him, she was,' continued Mr Frog. He sighed wistfully. 'Just my type, that one. Ah, there was a time—'

'So she had a book with her?' Lulu interrupted.

'You bet!' said Mr Frog, burping loudly again. 'Pardon me.'

'How could he!' Lulu couldn't help saying out loud. 'And...did you see this book?'

'My dear, I wasn't looking at the *book*. If you know what I mean.'

Lulu put her face in her hands. No, no, no!

So much for out-smarting the enemy; now all her efforts to protect *The Apple Star* had amounted to nothing. Why on earth hadn't she thought of this before?

Stale Chicken and Rice

It took Lulu a whole hour to reach home, but she managed to keep Aileen reassured by calling with excuses. She had to call three times in the end, because the journey was so much slower than the one going into town; the roads were clogged with people returning from work.

By the time she got home, Lulu felt she was about to explode. She had thought there was only one copy of *The Apple Star*, but clearly she had been mistaken...and now that Varaminta had her very own copy, did that mean it was *meant* for her, and so the recipes would work for her? Or did it still mean that it had fallen into the wrong hands and, as the book's introduction indicated, the recipes could therefore be harmful if used? Either way, the thought of what Varaminta might get up to now made Lulu shiver. And she was furious with Mister O, and frustrated she not been able to challenge him about what he had done.

All she could do was scrawl an angry note on a scrap of paper, and shove it through his letterbox. But this had done little to calm her rage, and now, although dinner was ready – and she was very hungry – there was one thing Lulu just had to do before eating. She went out into the back garden, shutting the door behind her. Clenching her fists, she marched to the very end of the garden, and let the rage spill out into an almighty yell.

How could Mister O betray her like this? The slimy creep! The low-down, dirty scumbag!

All of a sudden, her thoughts were interrupted by a slithery, undergrowthy sound; *splipple-ipple-ipp!* and she turned round to see that the Dum'zani plant was now growing even more vigorously than before she had harvested its cobs.

This reminder of her messed-up love-matching plan only made Lulu more furious. She marched over to the Dum'zani plant. 'And you can shut up as well!' she yelled, grabbing it and shaking it.

Splipple-ippy-squipp! went the plant, as it extended a new tentacle-like shoot, which wrapped itself around her right wrist.

'Aargh!' screamed Lulu, and she tried to tug her hand away, but the Dum'zani plant only tightened its grip, and sent out yet another shoot. This one squippled its way around her right leg. Lulu hopped and wriggled, but the plant was gaining strength by the minute, seemingly stimulated by the contact.

Lulu tried to wedge a finger between herself and the plant, but it clung on with all the determination of a boa constrictor. 'OK, I'm sorry!' Lulu cried. 'I didn't mean it, now let go!' The plant responded by sending out yet more shoots, *splipple-ipple-ippy-ipp-ipp*! Blue cobs were splipping forth all over the place. Lulu bit one, *crunch*, but this didn't stop it either. She bit some more, and some more, but the shoots just thickened around her, increasing in strength. As she struggled to free her right hand, her left wrist now became entangled in yet another shoot.

'Oh, blimey!' gasped Lulu. 'HELP!'

Then she felt an even stranger sensation, a feeling of weightlessness. She looked down, and realised that her feet were no longer touching the ground; the Dum'zani plant was actually *lifting her up*.

'Strewth, what the heck is going on?' said Aileen, emerging at last from the kitchen.

Lulu craned her head around to look at her, and tried to act normal. 'Ha ha! I was just having a game, and—'

Aileen was white as a sheet. She held up her hands. 'Don't move,' she ordered, 'I'll be right back!'

'I'm not going anywhere!' replied Lulu, unable now to conceal the panic in her voice.

Aileen disappeared into the kitchen, then returned wielding a large kitchen knife. 'Crikey, what on earth is this thing?' she exclaimed, as she valiantly sliced at the plant with the knife. 'Now hold still, we don't want any accidents, do we?'

The look of steely determination on Aileen's face as she stabbed and chiselled, like a chivalrous knight rescuing a damsel in distress, sudddenly made Lulu burst into hysterical laughter. The relief she felt at the gradual slackening of the tentacles around her only made her laugh more, and as she was finally released, she collapsed in a heap on the ground and laughed and laughed.

'Phew! You wanna get Costa to do something about that thing,' said Aileen, wiping the sweat from her brow. 'Blimey, I never saw anything like it! How on earth did you get tangled up like that, Lu?'

Lulu was still laughing uncontrollably. Eventually she calmed down, and sat up on her knees. She felt a new lightness, an inexplicable...happiness. She hugged Aileen's legs. 'Oh, you're so *great*, Aileen!'

'Get outta here!' said Aileen, laughing. 'Come on, kid, let's eat.'

Lulu let go and slowly got to her feet. She couldn't

fathom why, but in spite of everything – the appalling disaster with Dad and the Cupid Cakes, Mister O's betrayal with Varaminta and *The Apple Star* – she was quite overcome by a sense of the sheer gorgeousness of everything. 'Oh, Aileen, how I love this garden!' she exclaimed. She was aware that she sounded soppy but found she couldn't help herself.

'Are you kidding?' joked Aileen. 'It's just been attacking you!'

Lulu was so swept along by her elation, she didn't hear. 'Trees!' she exclaimed. 'Aren't trees just amazing? I *love* them!' She ran to the apple tree and hugged it.

'Oh boy,' said Aileen, shaking her head. 'OK, kid, get yourself inside and have some supper, before I phone the funny farm.'

'What's for supper?' asked Lulu.

'Chicken and rice,' said Aileen. 'Getting staler by the minute.'

'I LOVE chicken and rice!' squealed Lulu ecstatically, throwing her arms around Aileen once more. 'You are so *lovely* to make chicken and rice!'

Cornflakes and Toast

Lulu leaped out of bed the next morning, elated. She couldn't wait to get to school, it was just so wonderful and scintillating after all. And they had another rehearsal after school – fab!

At school, Lulu beamed at everyone, even Zena Lemon, who stuck her tongue out in response. At breaktime, Lulu ran up to Frenchy and hugged her. 'You are the best friend that anyone ever had in the whole world!'

'Steady on,' laughed Frenchy. 'You're awfully happy today. What happened?'

'Nothing!' said Lulu brightly. 'You're just great, that's all,' she added, smiling adoringly.

Frenchy took her aside, away from the others. 'Did you get the ingredient for the Anti-Dote, is that why you're so pleased?'

'The what? Oh, no. Hey, isn't Miss Broccoli brilliant? I loved the way she explained all that stuff about algebra today.'

Frenchy reached out and touched Lulu's forehead. 'Are you feeling OK?'

Lulu laughed. 'Oh, Frenchy, you look so serious! I love serious people.'

Frenchy gave Lulu a long, hard look and adjusted her spectacles. 'So,' she said at last, 'how was the piano lesson?'

'Oh! Didn't go,' said Lulu casually.

'How come?'

'You know who I bumped into? Torquil! Oh, and guess what? Varaminta went to Mister O's bookshop and got him to give her another copy of *The Apple Star*. Oh, look, there's Glynnie. Darling, *darling* Glynnie! Hiya!' She waved frantically.

Frenchy shot Lulu a severe look, then grabbed her by the shoulders. '*"Darling?!"* Lu, what's got into you? You're scaring me!' She dragged Lulu off to a secluded corner. 'Lu, what have you eaten in the last twenty-four hours?'

'What have I eaten?' echoed Lulu, frowning. Then she grinned. 'Oh, is this a game? I *love* games!'

'Yes, that's right, it's a game,' said Frenchy. 'So come on, what have you eaten?'

'Well, this morning I had cornflakes and toast. Is this the one where you say, "This morning I had cornflakes and toast *and* an egg," and so on? I love memory games!'

'No,' said Frenchy. 'What did you have last night?'

'Hey, isn't it your turn?'

'Not yet,' said Frenchy, sternly. 'Come on, what did you have last night?'

'Well, I had this lovely chicken and rice thing that Aileen does, but she had to warm it up because I was late getting back from Mister O's – oh, and then there was the accident with the Dum'zani plant. You wouldn't believe the way it's growing; I love that plant, it's so amazing!'

'What sort of accident?' pressed Frenchy.

'Oh, it's just I was tangled up in it, so Aileen had to set me free. Boy, that thing is strong! I love strong plants, don't you? I tell you, I was tugging and biting—'

'Biting? Did you say biting?'

'Yes, and it got hold of my—'

'Oh boy, that explains it,' sighed Frenchy.

'Explains what?'

'Lu, you *ate* the Dum'zani plant! Don't you realise what that means?'

'Ooh!' said Lulu, clapping her hand to her mouth.

'Remember what you told me? About how it makes you super-happy, makes you want to hug everyone and tell them you love them?'

Lulu stared at her, wide-eyed. She nodded vigorously.

'Lu, you're going to need that Anti-Dote too – I'm sure it will cure you as well.'

Lulu pouted like a chocolate-deprived four-year-old. 'Oo-oh!'

'Lu, you've got to take it – this *much* happiness isn't natural! Look, just keep your mouth shut during lessons today, OK? And I'll tell Mr Drinkmoore you couldn't make it to the rehearsal. I'm bringing *The Apple Star* back to you tonight,' said Frenchy. 'Have you got that last ingredient yet?'

Lulu shrugged petulantly.

'Well, check...no, *I'll* check. It should be there, it's Thursday; didn't you tell me it was coming on Thursday? But if it's not there I'll go to Cassandra's myself and get it.'

'All right, all right, I'll check,' said Lulu, sulkily.

'Lu, have you forgotten about your dad? You've got to get him back to normal again. Crikey, you're so busy dancing around on Planet Happy, you seem to have forgotten all about him, not to mention any other mischief Varaminta might get up to with *The Apple Star*. You've got to come back to the real world, Lu. And quick.'

Cool Sorbet

Lulu didn't feel like coming back to the real world; she was enjoying Planet Happy way too much. But Frenchy was getting crosser and crosser with her, and when she had delivered *The Apple Star* back to Lulu at the end of the day, she'd said, 'I only wish I could make the Anti-Dote myself, but it won't work properly if I do, and you know it. So do it, Louisa.'

Frenchy had never, ever called Lulu by her full name.

Lulu set out all the Candy-Coated Anti-Dote ingredients on the kitchen table; Cassandra had indeed delivered the milk-white Sha-Fu honey as promised, along with some useful pieces of information about all the ingredients. Each had an opposing effect to that of an ingredient in the Cupid Cakes recipe; the Chaste-Tree fruit, for example, cancelled out the effect of the Heartsease essence, so that the eater hardly even noticed the person they had previously found captivatingly beautiful. The Cankerblossom reversed the touchy-feely, love-everything effect of the Dum'zani corn, giving the eater a more jaded but realistic view of the world in general.

The recipe warned that accurate measurement was most important, otherwise things could go too much the other way, resulting in revulsion, loathing and misery. For the same reason, Lulu was instructed to take great care not to overdo the portion size. And now she was all set: Dad was out again, and Aileen was watching a film with Phil. She had wanted Lulu to join them, but Lulu had feigned disinterest. Not easy, because she absolutely *loved* Aileen and Phil to bits, and she *adored* watching films. But she loved Frenchy too, and that meant she had to fulfil her promise.

The Candy-Coated Anti-Dote, it turned out, was a frozen concoction like a sorbet, and quite simple to make. All Lulu had to do was whisk the whites of the penguins' eggs (whose coldness cooled the ardour of the doves' eggs) then stir in the finely-chopped Chaste-Tree Fruit, the Cankerblossom (not a flower, but the dried, powdered extract of a kind of worm) and the Sha-fu honey, made by very annoyed bees. The bees would have been annnoyed, Cassandra's notes explained, because the Chinese plant they make their honey from whirls its leaves about like fans, making the pollen-collecting a most frustrating and breezy business. This honey, read Lulu, was therefore quite rare, but most effective for the cooling of passions, rather as a fan cools the blood. She had to add a mere drop of cocoa-grape wine, to make Dad forget the forgetting induced in him by the same ingredient in the Cupid Cakes. Finally, she added the special anti-dote ingredient for Pisces, Dad's sign; chopped Hindering Knotgrass, a fragrant, lemony weed, especially effective for staunching the torrential passions that people of watery signs were particularly given to. Luckily, Lulu, being a Cancerian, was also a water sign, so she didn't need a different ingredient.

Once everything was mixed – into a pale, speckled greeny-yellow slush – Lulu noticed that a ghostly chill surrounded her. She found it a rather creepy feeling and quickly put the mixture away in the freezer, after which the room temperature returned to normal.

Later, because the Anti-Dote did have quite a strange flavour, she would need to serve it covered with whatever ice-cream toppings came to hand, the sweeter the better. She would have to wait two hours, though, before it was frozen and she could eat some. Two hours left of this lovely, warm feeling; then back to reality. Lulu sighed, put the Anti-Dote in the freezer, and restored *The Apple Star* to its hiding place in the encyclopedia; it felt good to have it home again. Then she went to join Aileen and Phil.

*

Lulu awoke at five o'clock the next morning, consumed with dread. After eating the Anti-Dote sorbet the night before, all the awful realities were coming back to her; Mister O's betrayal...what on earth was going to happen, now that Varaminta had her very own copy of *The Apple Star*? Then there was Dad; she hadn't even seen him last night, no doubt he'd had another secret date with the dreaded V-woman. And Lulu still had to find a way of getting him to eat the Anti-Dote.

Then she remembered the play; it was Friday already. With everything else that had been going on, Lulu hadn't focused on the fact that it was the dress rehearsal tonight, and performances tomorrow and Sunday. Her belly did a little flip inside. How was she possibly going to cope?

She would need sleep; it was all going to use up a lot of energy. She shut her eyes tightly, and pulled the duvet over her head, but it was no use. She was very, very awake.

Lulu had to wait over two hours for Dad to get up;

it felt like two days. She lay listening to the sounds of first the birds, then the milkman, then Costa the gardener arriving for his morning's work.

Finally, Dad emerged. Lulu joined him in the kitchen for breakfast. 'So where'd you go last night?' she asked.

Dad had made his favourite muesli-and-banana breakfast, but was just toying with it. 'Oh, nowhere special,' he said, peering at his spoonful of cereal as if he'd never seen such a thing before.

Lulu missed Normal Dad so badly, it gave her a pain in the chest. She wondered if it wasn't too early in the day for the Anti-Dote. 'How about some sorbet?' she suggested brightly, diving for the freezer.

Dad frowned at her. 'For breakfast?'

'Why not?' said Lulu, taking out the Anti-Dote. 'You eat fruit for breakfast, so why not *frozen*—'

She was interrupted by a strange cry from the back garden. Lulu peered out of the window and saw Costa wrestling with the Dum'zani plant. It was now about three metres tall, and its branches were beginning to strangle the neighbouring apple tree. Lulu groaned; she had meant to see what advice *The Apple Star* gave about keeping the crazy plant under control, but once again, she'd completely forgotten about it. Costa was now swearing at it very loudly in Greek. Oh, good grief, she thought, soon the whole neighbourhood will know about my magical plants!

Lulu turned back to speak to Dad, but he was gone. Another missed chance. She ran up to get *The Apple Star*, and quickly consulted its appendix. She found the 'Care of Your Plants' section and looked under 'Dum'zani':

> *Not for nothing is this plant named after the love god of the Sumerians, who first discovered it; its passion knows no bounds. It grows rampantly, and will take over your entire garden if you are not careful. If you intend to keep the plant for any length of time, therefore, you must confine it to a pot.*

Bit late for that! thought Lulu. But nor did she want it killed off; she found she had become very fond of it. She read on:

> *If you need to reduce your Dum'zani plant, beware; it loves human contact, so you must avoid touching it as much as possible. It is capable of locking you in an embrace that is very hard to escape from. Should this happen, the most effective remedy is to*

*feed the plant's roots with any one of the
anti-dote recipes in this book.*

Lulu snapped the book shut, hid it back inside the
encyclopedia, and ran downstairs. She grabbed the
Anti-Dote from the freezer, and reached the garden
just in time. Costa was wearing a big black dustbin
liner; his nose and mouth were covered with a
tea-towel, and over his eyes he wore Lulu's swimming
goggles. He had dug out her old Ultra Soaker water
cannon from the garden shed, and was pumping it up,
ready for action, while hurling Greek abuse at the
Dum'zani plant. He looked so preposterous, it took a
moment for Lulu to realise what was happening; then
she saw at his feet, a box of super-strength weed-killer.

'Stop!' she cried.

Costa went on pumping angrily. 'Is crazy weed, got
to kill—'

'NO!' shrieked Lulu. She ran forward, clutching the
plastic box of Anti-Dote, and stepped into the line of
fire. '*Please*, wait! I have just the thing!' She bent
down, scooped out some of the Anti-Dote with her
fingers, and smooshed it around the roots of the plant.
Immediately, it made a little sound, like a faint dog's
whimper, and relaxed. 'There!' said Lulu,
triumphantly. 'It won't attack any more, I promise.'

Carrots

8B's classroom had never been in such chaos. Everything had been brought in for the dress rehearsal, and the room was crammed with clothing rails, backpacks and plastic bags. Cast members in Shakespearean costume were crunching crisps, slurping cola and discussing which DVD to watch. Frantic mothers and teachers flitted around, hastily fastening zips, applying rouge, and generally trying to ensure that everything and everyone was where they were supposed to be.

After dressing, Lulu had retreated to the cloakrooms with Frenchy, so that she could bring her up to date on developments back home. '...So I used the Anti-Dote on the plant, and it worked!' she concluded.

'I hope you've kept some to use on your dad,' said Frenchy.

'Of course I have!' said Lulu. 'I'm not daft.'

Frenchy laughed. 'Oh, Lu, you were before! You were all, "Hello, lovely pencil. Aren't rulers brilliant?" You were doolally!'

Lulu grimaced with embarrassment as she remembered her behaviour. 'Yeah, well, I'm me again now. But Dad,' she sighed, 'he's still doolally. I don't know when I'll get the chance to give it to him; he's so fixated he's not interested in anything else, not even food.'

'Crikey, Lu, we've got to figure out what we're going to do about Varaminta too, now she's got that book. Have you heard anything from Mister O?'

'Ha! Not a peep.'

'Lu? Oh, there you are,' said Glynnie, appearing round the corner.

Lulu turned and gasped. 'Oh, Glyn, you look amazing!'

Glynnie gave a twirl. The high-waisted chiffon dress had extra-long, transparent sleeves, and its layered skirts trailed along the ground. Its pale yellow fabric was embroidered with pearls and sequins, and contrasted deliciously with Glynnie's caramel-coloured skin. Her already luxuriant hair was enhanced with extensions in glistening copper and bronze, and decorated with lots of little yellow fabric flowers. The effect was wonderfully romantic.

'Beautiful,' agreed Frenchy.

Glynnie smiled shyly. 'Thanks. Just came to say our scene's coming up soon, Lu. Mr Drinkmoore wants us waiting in the wings.'

'Oh, thanks,' said Lulu. 'Now, you're sure you're OK without your glasses?'

'I'm fine,' said Glynnie coolly. 'Don't worry. I'm beginning to think you were right about the carrots.'

*

'And, lights!' called Mr Drinkmoore. 'Numbers seven and eight up a bit...that's great, lovely colours. All right, enter Oberon stage right – wait, Titania...OK, enter Titania stage left.'

Lulu watched as Glynnie stepped forward, holding up her skirts. Then, all of a sudden, Glynnie lurched forward, 'AAARGH!' and collapsed in a heap on the stage. Everyone rushed over. Frenchy, and the other fairies who were following their queen, crowded round.

'Glyn, are you all right?' asked Frenchy, crouching beside her.

Glynnie was doubled up, clutching her leg. All she could say was '*Oww! Oww!*', and her face was scrunched with pain.

'She's really hurt,' said Mr Drinkmoore. His eye

followed the path Glynnie had just taken, and rested on the length of thick black wiring that was rigged up for the lighting. He went over and raised it with a finger. 'Why isn't this taped down?'

Jake Hershey scratched his head in an attempt to conceal a surreptitious concerned glance in Glynnie's direction. 'I thought I *had* taped it down,' he protested. 'I coulda sworn...'

'Do you realise how dangerous this is?' barked Mr Drinkmoore.

'Please, sir,' came a voice from behind Lulu. Zena Lemon stepped forward.

Please sir? thought Lulu; since when was Zena so polite to the teachers?

'I'm not being mean or nuffink,' went on Zena, 'but Galinda, y'know, she's s'posed to wear glasses. She keeps fallin' over fings, 'cos she don't want to wear 'em. So it ain't Jake's fault.'

Chantrelle Portobello and the other members of Zena's gang backed her up with a chorus of 'yeah's.

Lulu narrowed her eyes at Zena; this was all highly suspicious.

Fried Fish Fight

'Urrgh, I'm fried,' sighed Lulu, flopping onto the couch. 'What a day!'

'All right, missus,' said Aileen. 'Since it is nine o'clock, I'll make an exception and bring your dinner here.'

'Oh, thank you! Where's Phil?'

Aileen winced. 'Me an' him are cooling it a bit right now.'

'Oh.'

'Your dad just got home a little while ago,' said Aileen, quickly changing the subject. 'He's upstairs, changing.'

At last! thought Lulu. I'll finally get the chance to give him the Anti-Dote.

Right on cue, he appeared at the doorway. 'Hi, Dad,' said Lulu.

'Mmm, hi,' said Dad. As was usual these days, he looked as if he had lost something. Lulu watched as he sat down with his briefcase and opened it up, without even asking her about her day.

Aileen came in with two plates of fish and chips. 'Thought you might like some of this, Michael, since you haven't eaten yet.'

Dad looked up from behind his briefcase. 'Oh. Thanks.' He closed the briefcase, put it on the floor, and began to eat. Showing interest in food at last, thought Lulu, encouraged. Perhaps he would have the Anti-Dote for dessert.

Aileen sat beside Lulu. 'So,' she said, patting her on the leg, 'all ready for your big day?'

'Yes,' said Lulu loudly, sending a pointed look in Dad's direction, something he failed to notice. 'Pretty much. Although it looks as if Titania's got a sprained ankle.'

'Oh, no, that's too bad!' said Aileen. 'Hey, you're not the understudy, are you?'

Lulu, chewing a mouthful of fish, shook her head. 'No understudies. She'll have to do it.'

'Ouch, poor girl,' said Aileen. 'Ooh, but I'm so looking forward to seeing this!' she added, excitedly. 'Aren't you, Michael?'

Dad looked up from his fish and chips. 'Hmmm?'

'Aren't you excited about seeing your daughter in this play?'

Dad looked blank. 'Play?'

Lulu felt the rage rising inside her. 'You

haven't forgotten, Dad?'

'We planned to go *tomorrow*, Michael,' said Aileen, looking pretty angry herself.

'Oh!' said Dad, a light switching on in his brain. '*Romeo and Juliet*, right?'

'Dad!'

Aileen stood up. 'I've got to go home,' she announced suddenly. Lulu saw that she was shaking. She watched, dumbfounded, as Aileen marched out to the hall. She hadn't seen her this angry since the day Aileen had confronted Varaminta over her appalling treatment of Lulu on her birthday.

Aileen promptly returned. 'It's *A Midsummer Night's Dream*, Michael, and it's at three o'clock tomorrow. I hope you bought the tickets, like you said you would?'

'Ah, that. Uh—'

'Oh boy!' said Aileen, shaking her head. 'Don't worry, kid,' she added, kissing Lulu on the forehead. 'We'll work something out.' She turned back to Dad and said stonily, 'Goodbye, Michael.'

Lulu heard the front door slam shut, and felt as if she were going to cry. The thought of Dad and Aileen falling out with each other was unbearable. And Lulu was so tired, so fed up of constantly having to remind herself that it was her own fault he was behaving this way; how dare he forget about the play! She pushed away her plate of half-eaten fish and chips; she was not in the least bit hungry now.

'Noodle, I'm sorry, I—' Dad began.

'Yeah, right, you're sorry!' Lulu butted in. 'Well, sorry's not enough! I mean, what planet are you on?' She felt a twinge of guilt as she said this. What a hypocrite I am, she thought; I had to be talked down from Planet Happy myself! But the rage had let loose now, and all the pent-up emotion – about Dad, but also about Varaminta, Torquil, Mister O's betrayal – it all came flooding out. 'How *could* you just forget the play?'

Dad stood up. 'Now look here,' he retorted. 'I've been working very hard—'

'Oh right, sure thing, you've been *working*!' shrieked Lulu sarcastically, as she strode over towards him. 'Well, you want to know what I think of your rotten so-called work?' she said, grabbing his briefcase. 'This!' With that, she opened it up and dumped its contents onto the floor. She was not prepared for what she saw.

A poster. Postcards. A heavy art book – all revealing the same image. The picture was instantly familiar. Those big, dark eyes that followed you around the room. They had been following Lulu around her bedroom ever since she had bought the postcard at the art museum, and pinned it to her noticeboard. The elegant Spanish lady with the black *mantilla* over her head and the white gloves; the *Lady With a Fan* portrait.

And here she was now, gazing up at Lulu several times over, from all over the living-room floor. Lulu and her dad just stood in silence, staring.

'I wish that hadn't happened,' said Dad, flatly.

At first Lulu was confused; then, slowly, she began to chuckle...and to realise the mistake she had made. Dad hadn't fallen in love with the picture of Varaminta that day he'd eaten the Cupid Cake at all. No – it was as Lulu had first thought; he had taken a cake *before* he went upstairs to answer the phone. But the phone, she now remembered, had been in her bedroom, where she had left it after speaking to Frenchy – on her desk, right by her noticeboard. Until now, it hadn't even occurred to her that Dad might have seen another image before he saw the one of Varaminta. Leaving him madly, passionately in love with...a painting! *Lady With a Fan*...well, she certainly had one very devoted fan!

'Oh, Dad!' cried Lulu, and flung her arms around him, laughing. She squeezed him tight. 'Poor Dad!'

'Oh!' said Dad, surprised. 'I thought you were angry with me.'

'Dad,' said Lulu, hiccupping now, from all the mixed-up emotions. 'Hic! Let's go and have some...*hic!*...dessert! And I won't take no for an answer.'

Sour Lemon

'That's great, Aileen...see you later then!' Lulu's dad put the phone down, just as Lulu entered the kitchen for breakfast. 'Hey!' he greeted her, and went over to give her a big hug. 'Noodle, I've got some good news,' he said excitedly. 'The play's sold out, but I've been ringing around since last night, and it so happens there are a couple of returns. So Aileen and I will be there today, after all!'

'Brilliant!' cried Lulu, hugging him back. It felt wonderful to have him normal again. Then she remembered Aileen's anger from the night before. 'So has Aileen forgiven you?'

'Oh, I guess so,' said Dad, putting on the kettle. He scratched his head. 'What *was* the matter with me? Maybe it was stress, I don't know; never had anything like it happen to me before. I was obsessed! But now? Couldn't care less. Weird, huh?' He shook his head in wonder.

'Dad?'

'Yup?'

'Did you have a meeting with Varaminta the other day?'

'Oh,' groaned Dad, rolling his eyes. 'Yes. She's unbelievable, isn't she? I can't take a thing she says seriously, I'm afraid.'

'Why did you meet her then?'

'Well, that night at the art gallery? She went on and on about having some important business to discuss. I tried to get out of it, but she insisted. You want some hot chocolate?'

'No, thanks. So what *was* the "important business"?'

'Beats me,' said Dad, shaking his head. 'I wasn't really listening, to be honest. I've...been a bit preoccupied lately.'

I'll say you have, thought Lulu.

'What was it, now?' Dad asked himself, gazing into the distance as he opened the fridge. 'Something about a book? Something she wanted me to get for her. She must have forgotten it when she moved out.'

The Apple Star!

Dad took out the milk, and nudged the fridge door shut. 'Like I say, I had other things on my mind, and I just wanted her to go away, so I said, yeah, fine, whatever.'

Lulu thought back to her phone conversation with his secretary. 'And then you...went back to the office?'

'Yes...well, no. Actually, I went to the art museum, the one with the...you know.' Dad looked away, embarrassed.

'*Lady With a Fan*?'

'Uh-huh,' Dad admitted sheepishly.

'What, *all day*?'

Dad nodded slowly. 'Look, Noodle, I can't explain the way I've been lately...'

I can, thought Lulu. She pictured him, spending hour after hour gazing adoringly at the lady in the painting. Poor Dad! For five days, nothing and no one else had existed. *Love is blind*, as they say. Cassandra was right – wasn't she always? – he had indeed been suffering from unrequited love.

'...Anyway,' Dad was saying, 'all I know is, whatever was going on, I'm over it.'

Something still troubled Lulu. 'The DVD...' she said aloud.

'What DVD?'

'Oh, it's nothing really,' said Lulu. She didn't want Dad to know what she'd been thinking about him and Varaminta. 'I just noticed that Varaminta's "Sweet Nothings" DVD was in the player the other day.'

'Oh, did Phil bring it back?'

'Phil?'

'Mm...I let him have it to record his band on, there was loads of playing space left.'

'Oh,' said Lulu. 'He and Aileen must have been watching it...'

So that explained everything. She really needn't worry about Varaminta any more, where Dad was concerned. But as the day wore on, Lulu became plagued by a dark, heavy feeling...there was something she hadn't thought of... What sort of mischief would Varaminta get up to now that she had her very own copy of *The Apple Star*? Then an awful realisation dawned on her: Varaminta's copy might also have a coded message in it, just as Lulu's had, leading her to Cassandra for the ingredients. Torquil would have no trouble cracking the code, as Lulu and Frenchy had done.

Good grief, thought Lulu, why didn't I think of that before?

This time, Cassandra really might be in danger. But when she called Cassandra to warn her, she was once again unable to reach her.

Lulu forced herself to put it from her mind; with a play to put on, there was nothing more she could do for now.

*

This was it; the first performance. The nervous tension hung in the air, its acrid smell mingling with that of greasepaint and second-hand costumes.

Glynnie arrived on crutches, wearing her wonky glasses. Lulu's heart went out to her as she hobbled in, putting on a brave face.

'Wotcha, Glyn,' called Zena Lemon, loudly. 'Goin' in for the three-legged race, are ya?' Cue raucous laughter from the rest of her gang.

'Why don't you shut up, Zena?' retorted Lulu.

'Oo-ooh!' hooted Zena.

Lulu and Frenchy glared in disgust as Zena sauntered off, no doubt in search of Jake. 'That was no accident yesterday, was it?' said Frenchy.

'Just what I was thinking,' agreed Lulu. 'I bet Jake did tape that wire down. Zena probably unstuck it and hid the roll of tape.'

'Yeah, she probably yanked the wire, as well,' said Frenchy.

But they could prove nothing...and, as it turned out, they didn't need to: Mr Drinkmoore had some news. 'Right, we've got everything worked out, Glynnie,' he announced jovially, 'and you've nothing to worry about.'

Zena's smirk turned sour.

Everyone followed as Mr Drinkmoore led Glynnie to where Jake Hershey was putting the finishing touches to a mound covered with fake grass and daisies. 'Jake and I rigged this up this morning,' said Mr Drinkmoore. 'Go ahead, take a seat!' he added, gesturing to Glynnie.

Glynnie shifted herself awkwardly towards it, then flopped down. The mound supported her in a graceful, semi-reclined position. 'Ooh, this is comfy!' she enthused.

Zena scowled.

'Excellent!' said Mr Drinkmoore. 'Now, you won't be needing these,' he added, removing Glynnie's spectacles.

Glynnie looked puzzled. 'You mean, I'm to stay seated the whole time I'm on?'

'That's right,' said Mr Drinkmoore, triumphantly. 'Just like the legendary Sarah Bernhardt. Famous stage actress a hundred years ago; she had a leg amputated, but that never stopped her. She went right on performing, and the audiences loved her more than ever!'

Zena's scowl was now so extreme, she reminded Lulu of a particularly frightful gargoyle.

Glynnie looked up at Jake Hershey, her lovely black eyes wide with admiration. 'You made this, just this morning?'

'Uh, yeah,' muttered Jake into his turned-up collar.

'Thank you, Jake,' said Glynnie. 'That's really kind!'

Jake turned crimson. He shrugged. ''Sall right.'

Glynnie smiled radiantly at him, in a way she had never done before. Short-sighted though she was, she was no longer blind to the charms of Jake Hershey.

Lulu swore she could actually see steam rising from Zena Lemon.

Beauty Drink

On the floor of the stage lay two girls and two boys; four characters who, thanks to Puck's magical meddling, had experienced the confusion, pain and anguish of messed-up love matches. Now, at last, help was at hand as Puck knelt beside one of the boys.

'On the ground, sleep sound. I'll apply, to your eye, gentle lover, remedy.' So saying, he pretended to squeeze the antidote into the boy's eyes. 'And the country proverb known, that every man should take his own, in your waking shall be shown. Jack shall have Jill, nought shall go ill. The man shall have his mare again, and all shall be well.'

The curtain came down for the interval, prompting a round of applause.

'I'm going to go say hello to Mum and Dad,' said Frenchy, happily. '*Mum and Dad*...I love how that sounds!'

Lulu's dad was full of praise for her performance.

'Yeah, you're doing really well, kid,' agreed Aileen.

'Thanks,' said Lulu. 'And how about Glynnie! Isn't she—' Suddenly, she caught sight of Torquil. Her jaw dropped. 'Oh, no!'

He was coming towards them, and beside him was...someone the same height as Varaminta, with the same clothes as Varaminta, the same hairstyle, everything, except for one big difference: she looked *twenty years younger*. Her skin was flawless, even though – most unlike her – she wore barely any make-up. Her hair had a natural bounce and gloss to it, and her face was plumper and prettier. Her eyes sparkled beneath silky lashes.

Dad turned, and dropped his programme. 'Varaminta?'

Aileen, too, gaped in disbelief.

'Hello, Michael!' the girl-woman chuckled. Even her laugh had a youthfulness to it; it was astounding. 'Yes, it really is me! Hello, *Loo-Wheezer*,' she added, turning to Lulu with a spiteful glint in her eye. *That* hadn't changed.

Torquil smirked at Lulu, a look that said, 'I told you so.'

Varaminta waited until Dad had absorbed the full impact of her astonishing appearance, then said, 'You're going to wish you'd stayed with me, Michael. Do I look ravishing to you? Well, that's just for starters...I'm going to be *rich*, Michael; very, very rich. Minty's about to make a mint! Ha ha!' She laughed uproariously at her own joke.

'*Nothing* could make me wish I'd stayed with you, Varaminta,' Dad snarled. 'Least of all money.' He took Lulu's hand, and turned to leave. 'And by the way,' he added, rounding once more on Varaminta in disgust, 'no amount of plastic surgery can ever transform an ugly soul.'

'You said it, Michael, *whoo*!' howled Aileen, slapping him on the back with approval.

'Ha!' laughed Varaminta, as they walked away. 'Who said anything about plastic surgery?'

'Ladies and gentlemen!' came Mr Drinkmoore's voice over the PA system. He mounted the stage, carrying a basket wrapped in red cellophane and tied with a fat red ribbon. 'As you probably know, Ferretsmore School is holding a prize draw at the end of today and tomorrow's performances. And I'm delighted to tell you that, quite at the last minute, the model and celebrity author Varaminta le Bone has presented us with this most remarkable first prize, and offered to make the draw...'

Oh, no! thought Lulu.

'...And this hamper, I'm told, contains six months' supply of, let me get this right, a "Natural Super-Vitamin-Fortified Detoxifying And Beautifying

Health-Elixir Concentrated Juice Drink," which I am told works like *magic*! In fact, this is a sneak preview of a product line soon to be launched by Ms le Bone...'

Oh, good grief!

'...Who, if her appearance today is anything to go by, I think you'll agree, is on to something! So if you haven't already bought your raffle tickets, do go and buy some now; this is your last chance to win this fantastic prize!'

Lulu saw Varaminta shoot another gloating look back at Dad.

'Oh, that *woman*!' he growled, as he guided Lulu and Aileen swiftly in the direction of the snack bar. He sounded exactly as he had done the last time they'd seen Varaminta, and part of Lulu noted with joy that it was true: he really did despise her.

But the rest of her was sinking into a morass of gloom. A beautifying drink that 'works like *magic*'; could Varaminta really have succeeded in using a recipe from *The Apple Star* somehow? Lulu hadn't come across anything for making old people look younger, but then she hadn't really been interested in the section on physical problems. Whereas Varaminta would, of course, have gone straight for that. How typical that she should be motivated by vanity and greed. But how on earth could she have got hold of the ingredients? Not willingly from Cassandra, Lulu was sure of that. Could there be someone else? And who knew what else she might do now, armed with *The Apple Star* and, apparently, a source of ingredients? It was all Lulu's nightmares come true.

'Cheer up, kiddo, she can't harm you now,' said Aileen, noticing Lulu's fretful look as they joined the queue at the snack bar.

Oh, yes, she can, thought Lulu. She hadn't forgotten Varaminta's words in *Chow!* magazine, about how she intended to have her revenge. 'I know,' she said out loud to Aileen, 'but...um, I just need to talk to Frenchy, all right?'

'All right,' said Aileen. 'Can I get you anything?'

'Oh, no thanks,' said Lulu as she headed off. She took the quickest route back to the changing room, via the school grounds. But as she made her way through the loose crowd of parents who stood chatting in the afternoon sun, she had the feeling of being watched. Glancing around, she caught sight of none other than Mister O, sitting on a bench and waving at her, smiling. Lulu felt herself consumed afresh with rage. She marched over to him.

'Hello, Lulu,' said Mister O cheerfully. 'I've been looking for you. I got your note.'

For a moment, Lulu wondered how he had traced her, but there were more pressing questions on her mind.

'Uh-huh?' she said, hands on her hips. 'Well, considering what you did, you don't look too ashamed of yourself.'

'I can explain—' began Mister O.

'She's really got it in for me, and she'll use that book for evil purposes,' Lulu couldn't help interrupting, her voice growing more and more shrill. 'Yeah, and it's not just me who'll suffer. She's got a wicked son who'll stop at nothing to make money! They'll be in it together, just you watch. Do you have *any* idea how much damage you've done? Well?' she prompted, as he just watched her, saying nothing.

Mister O peered over his spectacles at her. 'You're assuming,' he said eventually, 'that the lady has the same book as you.'

Lulu was just getting into her stride. 'And I thought you were a friend! I thought...' She trailed off, as his words sunk in. 'She doesn't?'

'No, of course not,' said Mister O.

Lulu struggled to make sense of this. 'But if it's not...but she wanted *The Apple Star*...and...' Lulu pointed in the direction of the school hall.

'I think you're forgetting one very important thing, young lady.'

'What's that?'

Mister O leaned forward. 'I told you before, nobody *ever* finds a book in my shop,' he said. 'It's impossible! If they come in and say, "Have you got so-and-so?", I just tell them I haven't the foggiest. And it's true,' he chuckled, scratching his shiny head, 'I never have a clue. So it was with madam over there.'

Lulu wasn't impressed with this show of funny-old-man innocence, as she saw it. 'Well, how come she's just been boasting about how rich she's going to be, huh? Where did she get these "magic" beauty products from, all of a sudden? And I happen to know she was *ecstatic* when she came out of your shop. Mr Frog saw what happened—'

'Mr Frog?'

'The man outside the pub: he told me she was clutching a book like a prize possession and *hugging* you – oh, yes, don't think I don't know about that!'

Mister O waited patiently for Lulu to finish. 'It's the book that found her, child. Mine is the shop where books find their people, not the other way round.'

'Yes I know, but—'

'Exactly. So the book she was carrying was, I can assure you, her book, the book that found her, and none other.'

Lulu frowned. 'So if it's not...well, what is it, then?'

'Its title is *The Secret of Eternal Youth*.'

Lulu gasped. Everything suddenly slotted into place, like the final piece of a jigsaw puzzle. And now she was embarrassed. 'I'm so sorry, I didn't realise. I thought—'

'That's not all,' said Mister O. 'There's something about that book that she doesn't know.'

'There is?'

'Mm-hm,' said Mister O, nodding. 'You see, Lulu, people who end up in my shop always do so because they are searching for something. Take you, for example. Ah, you thought you were running *away*, but the fact is, nobody ever ran away from one thing, who wasn't looking for another. You may have found some of what you were searching for already...'

'Well, yes...'

'...But not everything. I can tell you have more to learn.'

Lulu lowered her head. She had to admit she did.

'You will, though, you will. Then there are those like...that woman.' Mister O shook his head sadly. 'Her sort will never learn. What they are searching for is...simply the wrong thing. You see, unlike your book, hers is a fraud. One fraud will always find another, you know. She's got the book she deserves.'

'Oh my...' Lulu paused. 'So does that mean the Super-Vitamin whatsit beauty drink, whatever it's made of...?'

'Total sham,' said Mister O, nodding. 'Of course, she doesn't know that. But it'll all backfire on her before too long.'

Hamper of Goodies

Lulu felt a whole combination of emotions, all at once. Relief, that Varaminta didn't have her own version of *The Apple Star* after all, but something fake. Remorse, for having been so quick to judge Mister O, and for being so wrong. Worry, because although Varaminta deserved to have things backfire on her, Lulu was beginning to realise that those 'miracle beauty products' would have to be withdrawn immmediately. Who knew just what would go wrong? It was one thing for something ghastly to happen to Varaminta, but quite another when someone completely innocent was involved...

'Hey, kiddo, there you are!' called Aileen, coming towards them.

Lulu gave a start, and turned around. 'Oh, hi, sorry, I just got talking to...' She was about to introduce Mister O, but when she turned back to the bench, he had gone. '...Someone,' Lulu finished off, quizzically.

Mister O had to be far more nimble on his feet than she imagined; there was no sign of him anywhere.

Dad appeared at Aileen's side. 'You'd better get backstage, Noodle,' he said. 'They're about to start the second act.'

'Oh, right!' said Lulu. 'See you later, then.' She reached up and kissed Dad on the cheek, and ran back into the auditorium. Before she went backstage, Lulu felt she should try to say something to Varaminta. Then she thought, hang on, who am I kidding? Varaminta wasn't going to believe anything she told her, least of all something she didn't want to hear...

Lulu slowed down, wondering what to do next. She didn't have to wonder for long; as she entered the lobby there, on a table, sat the red-ribboned hamper. Before she knew what she was doing, Lulu had grabbed it and dived into the nearest room, the biology lab. A model of a human skeleton stood near the doorway; she shifted it on its stand and wedged it against the door, then glanced around the room. She would have to hide the hamper – or better still, destroy it. But no sooner had she begun to rip at the red cellophane, than there was a rattle as someone tried to open the classroom door.

'Louisa!' growled Varaminta. 'I know you're in there!' *Rattle, rattle.*

Hide! thought Lulu. She shoved the hamper into one of the long, low cupboards that lined the lab – the emptiest one she could find – then climbed in after it and slid the door shut as far as she could.

There was a crash and a clatter, and now Varaminta was inside the lab – along with Torquil, by the sound of it. 'Right, you start over there, I'll take this end,' Varaminta instructed him. 'We know you're hiding, Louisa,' she called out. *Sshhft, sshft*, went the sliding doors.

There was only one thing for it. Lulu took the hamper, burst out of the cupboard and made a dash for the door. But the skeleton was in the way, and as she tried to move it, she felt a tight grip on her arm. She dropped the hamper, and Varaminta picked it up.

'All right, Poodle, the game's up!' gloated Torquil.

Lulu turned to face them both glaring down at her. 'It's not what you think!' she blurted. 'Look, I know all about your secret book, and there's something *you* should know.'

Varaminta looked down her nose at Lulu and sneered. 'Oh? And what would that be, hmmm?'

Lulu cleared her throat. 'It's a fraud. I knew you wouldn't believe me if I told you, so—'

'So you thought you'd sabotage the whole thing,' interrupted Varaminta, clutching the hamper tightly.

'Well, nice try, ha! Come on, Torquil.'

'It's true,' insisted Lulu. 'I saw Mister O, and—'

'Oh *right*,' said Torquil, sarcastically. 'And this would have nothing to do with us having something more valuable than you do, of course!'

'Pathetic!' spat Varaminta. 'Well, I wasn't born yesterday, you know...although, haha, I may look it!'

'You know I don't care what happens to *you*,' Lulu snapped back. 'You'll find out soon enough that I'm telling the truth. But you mustn't go out there and present that prize.'

Varaminta laughed so sharply at this, she made Lulu jump. 'Ha! Ordering me around now...that's very rich! Well it won't wash, madam. You've ruined my life once over, you won't do it again.'

'Yeah, y'know you still haven't paid her back for that, Mum,' sneered Torquil.

Varaminta seized him by the shoulder dramatically. 'Good heavens, you're right; I haven't, have I?' Her eyes narrowed. 'I think it's about time her little secret was out, don't you? About the precious recipe book! No point in keeping it secret any longer...we've got what we want now. Yes, I think it's time!'

'You can say what you like!' retorted Lulu, struggling to ignore the stomach-churning effect of Varaminta's remarks, as well as the familiar, acrid smell of her perfume. 'No one will believe you, and with good reason, because it's not true!'

She turned and ran off, her head spinning. Just when she thought everything was all right again – Varaminta no longer tracking down *The Apple Star*, Dad safe and back to normal, Varaminta quite possibly about to get her 'just desserts' – *The Apple Star* was in danger again.

Purple Sprouts

'Lu, I heard the announcement in the interval,' said Frenchy, as soon as they were able to grab a quiet moment backstage together during the second half. 'What's all this about a miracle vitamin beauty drink? Is that what I think it is?'

Lulu clutched her stomach. 'Oh, I feel ill!'

'Don't worry, Lu, it can't be that bad.'

'Yes it can,' hissed Lulu. 'She's going to tell all about *The Apple Star*!'

'Lu, she's not going to do that!' said Frenchy. 'Not now she's got a copy of her own. She'll want to keep it dead secret!'

'That's just it,' said Lulu, 'she hasn't got a copy!' She told Frenchy all about meeting Mister O, and everything he had told her. 'So you see,' she said finally, 'not only is some poor sucker going to get that dodgy hamper, but as far as Varaminta's concerned, she's got nothing to lose by spilling the beans.'

Frenchy blew a gum bubble, and it popped. 'Oh,' she said, ominously. For once, she didn't seem to have any brilliant ideas.

Then it was time for them to go on stage for the final scene. This is the best performance of my life, thought Lulu grimly, as she leaped and twirled this way and that with apparent carefree abandon, while her stomach was tied in knots. Then, as the fairies left the stage, Puck remained to deliver his closing speech, suggesting the whole story was nothing more than a dream. Lulu couldn't help wishing this was all a dream too. Instead of the elation she should have been feeling, with the play drawing successfully to a close, she felt as if she was having a dreadful nightmare.

Lulu drifted back on to the stage to take her bows at the sound of applause breaking out. Out of the corner of her eye, she noticed Jake helping Glynnie to her feet, holding on to her hand as she bowed, but it did nothing to lighten her mood. She caught sight of Dad and Aileen in the audience, beaming and applauding enthusiastically. She did her best to beam back, but could only manage a sort of chimpanzee grimace.

Then Mr Drinkmoore came on stage and, after a brief speech, instructed the cast to remain on the stage until after the draw. Then he introduced Varaminta.

Lulu thought her knees would give way beneath her. Varaminta came forward, bearing the gaily-wrapped and be-ribboned hamper. Lulu still couldn't get over how young she looked. Murmurings in the audience indicated that plenty of other people were also amazed.

'Before I draw the winning ticket,' announced Varaminta, 'a brief word about what's in this basket. As Mr Drinkmoore mentioned earlier, this is a sneak preview of a range of products that are, I can say with absolute certainty, no less than revolutionary! I think the results speak for themselves...'

More murmurings in the audience. Varaminta stepped forward, to give an even better view of her flawless face. 'Fourteen or forty...who can tell? Ladies, you see before you a wish come true!' This was greeted with a spontaneous burst of applause. 'Therefore it comes as no surprise,' Varaminta continued, raising her voice excitedly, 'that the raffle tickets have completely sold out, with the last few selling at many times the asking price!' There was another ripple of applause. Varaminta, apparently hot under the stage lights, dabbed at her brow with a tissue. '...It will be some time before clinical trials are completed,' she went on, 'which is why this is such an extraordinary opportunity to...' She took out another tissue, and wiped her neck. '...To be the first to...excuse me...'

There were further murmurs from the audience, although this time they sounded more like mutterings of concern.

'What's going on?' whispered Frenchy.

'Oh boy, here we go.' Lulu covered her face and peeked through her fingers, as it dawned on her what was happening. 'I think it's backfiring on her already!'

Varaminta attempted to continue. Her voice wavered a little. '...Well, without further ado, I think we should...'

All of a sudden, there was a *splip!* and Lulu froze. Oh, good grief, she thought; it couldn't be! Wide-eyed, she scanned this way and that, imagining her Dum'zani plant might actually have walked to school. But it wasn't the plant. Something else was growing...*sprouting*. And it was happening on Varaminta's face.

'*Aargh!*' Varaminta turned, and a moment later there was another *splipp!* as a gigantic purple spot erupted, smack in the middle of her right cheek. Then another. Varaminta was breaking out all over.

Splip, splip, splipp! Three more! Varaminta slapped at the huge pimples, consumed with horror.

There were stirrings and louder mutterings from the audience; some people were getting up to leave, others gazed on in stunned disbelief.

Then one mother said loudly, 'She's got the skin of a fourteen-year-old, all right!'

'Yeah, one with full-blown acne!' quipped her husband. This prompted nervous laughter from several other audience members. Lulu wondered what Mr Drinkmoore was making of all this, but there was no sign of him anywhere. Perhaps this would put Varaminta off making her revelation about *The Apple Star*, but Lulu didn't feel like sticking around to find out. She sought out Dad's face in the audience, and jerked her head towards the door. He nodded vigorously, and he and Aileen swiftly left their seats and headed down the aisle. Lulu began to sidle her way off the stage.

Varaminta had now taken her powder compact from her bag, and was frantically dabbing at her face in a desperate attempt to cover up the volcanic eruptions. She turned back to the audience. 'Heat rash!' she shrieked. 'Nothing to do with these fantastically effective products!'

'Pull the other one!' jeered a voice from the back.

As Dad and Aileen headed out of the doorway at the back of the auditorium, Mr Drinkmoore entered, a large glass of whisky in his hand. His jaw dropped. 'Somebody get the curtains, for Pete's sake!' he demanded. He downed his drink, wiped his mouth and advanced towards the stage.

Just as Lulu was about to escape, Torquil sprang forth from below the stage, grabbed her ankle and yanked her forward. 'Tell them, Mum!' he cried. 'Tell them now!'

The curtains swished shut in front of Varaminta, but she swooped through them and glared down at Lulu. Lit from below by the footlights, pimples pustulating and eyes on fire, she truly resembled a figure from a horror movie. Her arm shot out to point at Lulu as she yelled, 'This is all *her* doing! Nothing to do with my wonder youth drink at all! She's a meddler!' But hardly anyone was listening, and the few that were just gaped in disbelief. Varaminta struggled to make herself heard above all the commotion, raising her voice even more. 'She puts *spells* on people...she should be arrested, and her wicked recipe book should be *confiscated*!'

At that moment, the curtain behind her billowed forward, and the next thing Lulu knew, Jake's hand-made fairy queen mound emerged, and slid headlong into Varaminta, causing her to fall backwards onto it. The audience, already beginning to laugh at Varaminta's absurd accusations, exploded with mirth. Lulu just glimpsed Frenchy behind the mound before she was concealed again by the curtain.

Good old Frenchy! Lulu smiled as Mr Drinkmoore rushed forward to assist Varaminta.

Torquil's grip on Lulu's ankle slackened for a moment as he mounted the stage, and she seized the opportunity to pull her leg free. Yes! She managed to scramble her way behind the curtain and was just running off-stage when Torquil caught up with her again. He quickly grabbed hold of her arms in such a way that she couldn't move. 'This only makes it worse for you, *Poodle*,' he growled. 'Don't think you're getting away now!'

Suddenly, Jake Hershey came out of nowhere and pounced onto Torquil's back, but seconds later, he was flying through the air as Torquil, quick as a flicker, dispatched him with one arm, while still managing to keep hold of Lulu with the other. Lulu remembered with dismay that Torquil was *extremely good* at karate.

But what Torquil didn't see was Glynnie, as she now emerged from the wings...hobbling along with all her might and carrying the ass' head Bottom had worn in the play. Desperately, she lunged forward...and clamped it onto Torquil's head. Immediately his hands went up to push against it, and Lulu was freed. A dishevelled Jake leaped forward again and hung tightly onto the struggling Torquil, keeping the now fast-disintegrating påpier maché ass' head firmly in place.

Lulu rolled out of the way and got to her feet, dusting herself down. 'Thank you...thank you!' she gasped.

Frenchy, red-faced and flustered, made shoving movements with her hands. 'Get back to your dad...go! We'll let him go once you're safely out of the way. I'll see you later...go, go!'

'Uh...OK. Thanks!' said Lulu, stepping backwards. She turned and dashed back out into the auditorium to join the rapidly exiting crowd. The last thing she saw as she headed out of the door was Mr Drinkmoore leading Varaminta, face buried in her hands, off the stage...

BBQ Basking

Lulu lay spread-eagled on the grass next to Frenchy; moonbathing, as they liked to call it. This was such a delicious moment, Lulu wished she could capture it for ever, take a snapshot. To capture not just the beauty of the twilit garden, with the Moon and Venus shining in the darkening sky, but the smells, too; honeysuckle and jasmine, mingled with the perfume of her protective flowers and the smoky aroma of the barbecue. More than this, she wanted a snapshot of this feeling, that all was well again. The sheer relief that everything was back to normal, and that Varaminta had failed spectacularly in her efforts to reveal the secret of *The Apple Star* – ghastly though that scene had been.

Lulu took a deep breath of the warm night air. Beside her stood the Dum'zani plant, now neatly confined to a pot, its little cobs faded to white. It would take more tears to generate the powerful love-inducing blue ones, and Lulu had had enough of Cupid Cakes to last a lifetime, thank you. But the plant remained, a tamed ally as well as a reminder of what could go wrong with her magic, if she didn't take care to do exactly as the book told her. Mister O was right; she still had a great deal more to learn. She had been wrong about him, but most importantly, she had been wrong about Dad. She had doubted him, and now she knew she'd never make that mistake again. She was reminded once more of Cassandra's words, *If the Sun and Moon should doubt, they'd immediately go out.* Just because the Sun might sometimes be obscured by cloud – as Dad had been when Varaminta came into his life – it didn't mean it, or he, wasn't still as brilliant and true as ever.

And Lulu had been afraid, imagining all the things that might happen if she didn't take control of the situation; that fear, too, had been her enemy, making her act rashly and unwisely. *You have nothing to fear but fear itself...* Doubt and Fear, Lulu now realised, were two very nasty spectres that could lead you into an awful lot of trouble, if you let them. Once again, Cassandra – and Lulu's Truth Star – had been spot on.

Dad was sitting beside the glowing embers of the barbecue, talking to Jill, Jack and Aileen. 'Anyway, it hasn't done the school any harm,' Jack was saying. 'I heard they raised enough money from that draw to buy a new piano!'

'Well, that's something,' said Jill. 'I still can't get over how Varaminta just started breaking out like that, though. It was awful!'

'Ah, she'll be all right,' said Dad. 'She's tough as old boots! Looks as if that beauty drink thing of hers could use some serious testing, though. But of course, she couldn't wait to show off—'

'Show off to *you*,' remarked Aileen.

'Yeah,' agreed Jill, 'that's what it was all about, wasn't it?'

'Serves her right, if you ask me,' said Jack.

Tough as old boots, thought Lulu. Yes, Varaminta was nothing if not thick-skinned. 'Just like the Nemean lion!' she said aloud.

Frenchy gave a start. 'The what?'

'French,' said Lulu, propping herself up on one elbow, 'is it me, or does Varaminta keep popping up in my life like some monster out of Greek mythology?'

'Oh, don't say that!'

'No, really! This time around Varaminta was stalking Dad like a hungry lioness – like the Nemean Lion, from the Heracles myth – so thick-skinned that he was powerless in his attempts to fight her off—'

'Ah, except he wasn't, was he?' said Frenchy. '*You* gave your dad that power, without knowing it.'

'I did?'

'Sure you did. Think about it!' Frenchy rolled onto her front, leaned over and whispered the secret part in Lulu's ear. 'That little talk she had with him about getting hold of a certain book? Imagine if that had happened when he was normal! But your Cupid Cakes saw to it that he wasn't, didn't they?'

'Oh, yeah!' said Lulu. 'I did that. My cunning helped fight off the Nemean Lioness! *And* her monstrous ass-headed brute of a son!'

'What did you say, Lulu?' Dad called over.

'Oh, nothing,' Lulu replied. She flopped back onto the grass and chuckled.

'Hey, something just fell out of your pocket,' said Frenchy, pointing to the ground close to Lulu.

Lulu looked down. There, close to her trouser pocket, was a small, plastic zip-lock bag. She picked it up. Inside were what looked like some kind of seeds, and a hand-written note. Lulu moved closer to a nearby lantern and studied it. 'It's from Cassandra!' she whispered excitedly.

Frenchy huddled up to Lulu and they read it together:

DEAR LULU

CONGRATULATIONS! YOU HAVE SUCCESSFULLY CARRIED OUT THREE RECIPES (ALTHOUGH RECIPE NO. 2 DID NOT HAVE THE DESIRED EFFECT, IT WAS NEVERTHELESS DONE WITH GOOD INTENT AND HAD A HAPPY OUTCOME). YOUR SUCCESS HAS BEEN DUE TO THE CONVICTION YOU HAVE DEMONSTRATED, AND THE TALENT YOU HAVE SHOWN IN CREATIVE COOKING AND NURTURING YOUR PLANTS. THEREFORE, YOU QUALIFY TO MOVE UP TO THE NEXT GRADE OF RESPONSIBILITY, WHICH IS TO BUILD YOUR OWN PRIVATE STORE OF INGREDIENTS — IF YOU WISH TO DO SO. YOUR INHERITANCE OF *THE APPLE STAR* IS A LEGACY YOU SHOULD CONTINUE, AND THIS IS THE NEXT STEP IN THAT PROCESS. I VERY MUCH HOPE YOU WILL, AND ENCLOSE THESE SEEDS AS A GESTURE OF MY FAITH IN YOU. PLEASE PLANT THEM, AND WE WILL SPEAK AGAIN VERY SOON.

LOVE,

CASSANDRA

Lulu gasped. 'What do you know, I've qualified!' she giggled. 'I didn't even know I was doing a test in the first place!' Lulu was suddenly reminded of her horoscope too. 'A step forward' it had said, what if it had been referring to her sensible use of *The Apple Star* all along, she just hadn't seen it?

'How'd that note get there, then?' mused Frenchy.

Lulu shrugged. 'Cassandra could have been at the school today, I guess...'

'Hey, you know what? I thought I saw someone that looked like her,' said Frenchy, who had met Cassandra once before. 'Maybe it *was* her...she could have slipped into the changing room and put it in your pocket during the play.'

'Ha! Of course, that makes perfect sense,' said Lulu. 'She'd have wanted to keep an eye on things; she knew how worried I was. And it figures, because from her note she obviously knows Dad's back to normal. She probably saw what happened with Varaminta as well. Well, I'm glad she's all right. And she's forgiven me! I wasn't sure she ever would. Hey, just think, French, my very own store of goodies!'

'So you're not freaked out any more? I mean, you wanted nothing to do with this whole recipe malarkey for ages!'

'You know, I'm not. Not really...' Lulu thought for a moment, as she toyed with the bag of seeds. Being the owner of *The Apple Star* was not without its difficulties. Yet what was the point of having such a magical book, if she didn't use it? And she was eager to learn more; 'moving up to the next grade' had never been such an exciting prospect. Lulu gazed up at the sky, where the stars were just beginning to appear; one of them, she was sure, was her Truth Star. Yes, it seemed to say; you must go on... She felt sure it was what Mum would have wanted, too.

Lulu held up the bag and peered at the seeds. 'I wonder what these are for?'

'Guess you'll find out soon enough,' said Frenchy.

'Yes...' Lulu gave the Dum'zani plant an affectionate nudge with her finger; it responded with a corresponding lightness of touch, just curling a tendril around the finger. Soon, another plant would be added to her garden; then another, and another. What she would use them for, she had no idea yet. But the thought filled her with a delicious sense of anticipation.

And if she could ward off that thick-pelted lioness, Varaminta, and her wicked cub, Torquil – well, as Ambrosia May said in her book, anything and everything was possible.

The End